PRAISE FOR BITE RISK

'*Bite Risk* by the most talented S. J. Wills will have you turning each page feeling sheer horror and laughter.' **A. M. Dassu**

'Pure, thrilling brilliance!' **Louie Stowell**

'This high-concept dystopian tale with a werewolf twist has tension and scares galore and is perfect for fans of *Stranger Things* and *Big Bad Me*.' **Irish Independent**

'I inhaled this book. A concept that crackles, watertight world building, characters you care deeply about, & then the twists & turns …' **Nicola Penfold**

'Fun, gripping and deliciously gory.' **Amy McCaw**

'I devoured *Bite Risk* with ruthless ferocity, or perhaps the book devoured me – I'm not too sure!' **Sophie Kirtley**

'Smart, pacy, twists and turns with a hero who feels real. Exciting, thrilling but not too scary.' **Emma Norry**

'A gripping, fast-paced thriller.' **Nizrana Farook**

'*Bite Risk* sinks its claws into you and doesn't let go until its page-racing end.' **Maria Kuzniar**

'Fresh, exciting and just what teenagers everywhere need!' **Catherine Emmett**

'Incredible. Astonishing. Sweeps you away and afterwards, there is just SO much to think about.' **Rashmi Sirdeshpande**

'S. J. Wills proves a dab hand at world creation, sketching friendships and rivalries against a backdrop of post-disruption norm

Also by S. J. Wills:

Bite Risk
Bite Risk: Caught Dead

BITE

COLD BLOOD · COLD BLOOD · COLD BLO

RISK

S.J. WILLS

SIMON & SCHUSTER

London New York Amsterdam/Antwerp Sydney/Melbourne Toronto New Delhi

First published in Great Britain in 2025 by Simon & Schuster UK Ltd

Text copyright © 2025 S.J. Wills

1 3 5 7 9 10 8 6 4 2

Simon & Schuster UK Ltd
1st Floor, 222 Gray's Inn Road
London WC1X 8HB

www.simonandschuster.co.uk
www.simonandschuster.com.au
www.simonandschuster.co.in

Simon & Schuster Australia, Sydney
Simon & Schuster India, New Delhi

The authorised representative in the EEA is Simon & Schuster
Netherlands BV, Herculesplein 96, 3584 AA Utrecht, Netherlands.
info@simonandschuster.nl

A CIP catalogue record for this book
is available from the British Library.

PB ISBN 978-1-3985-2100-1
eBook ISBN 978-1-3985-2102-5
eAudio ISBN 978-1-3985-2101-8

Typeset in Archer by M Rules

Printed and Bound in the UK using 100% Renewable
Electricity at CPI Group (UK) Ltd

MIX
Paper | Supporting
responsible forestry
FSC
www.fsc.org
FSC® C013604

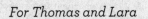

For Thomas and Lara

CHAPTER 1

Sel

Saturday 12 January

'Sel. *Sel.*'

I snap back to the room. Lucas Torres is leaning forward, elbows on his knees, frowning slightly.

'Sorry. Miles away.'

I grab the glass of water from the small table next to me and sip it, stalling. It takes me a couple of seconds to remember where I am.

Lucas's therapy office at the Wellness Centre. It looks out onto the misty parking area, the few cars rimed with frost, windows opaque. There's a crow pecking at something in the corner by the bins, its powerful beak stabbing and pulling, inky black head popping up to check its surroundings before getting back to work. My stomach rolls queasily as I realize what it's eating: a dead squirrel.

You can still just make out the space where a shipping crate once sat. That's where it happened – the bite that changed me, just a few months ago.

But the bite itself isn't what I was thinking of just now. In my mind, I was in the forest again. Images and sensations from recent Howl nights roll through me in waves – things I shouldn't be able to remember. I only had a few months as a normal Ripper, changing once a month to a wolfish beast along with the rest of the town. I would wake up in the morning after Howl night back in my human body, happy, but without a clue where I'd been or what I'd done. Not anymore. Ever since that bite, when that Howl night sunset arrives, I can watch as the hairs emerge from my skin as my limbs expand, shuddering with the power that courses through them.

I can decide where to go. I place my paws with intent and feel every stone under my toe pads. I hang out and wrestle with neighbours and acquaintances who, come dawn, don't have a clue they ever saw me.

And I always seek out Ingrid, because she was bitten by the mutated monster that we called the Revenant, too. Our *corpus pilori* – the virus that causes Turning for everyone else – has changed in response. We've taken to calling it *extra pilori*.

Corpus was easy – you just change and spend the night

happily playing as a Ripper. But *extra* needs management. It takes you by surprise.

'*Sel.* You're doing it again.' Lucas is patient, but I can tell he's getting frustrated. This is his actual paid job, now, but *my* sessions are free, because Mum is dead worried about my behaviour and he knows we don't have money to spare. He's a good guy, but he doesn't yet have the kind of training and experience that would enable him to crack me open and get me to spill my guts. It doesn't help that he's my best friend's dad, either.

I push myself straighter in the armchair, screwing my face up in the hope it'll keep my brain from wandering off again.

'Sorry, sorry. I'm … tired. This chair is really comfy. It's making me sleepy.'

I can't look Lucas in the eye. He's been through so much himself, and he wants to help. It's not his fault I'm lying to him.

'Let's talk about why you're constantly tired.' He checks the paper in front of him, with my blood test results. Nothing sinister has showed up, to my relief. 'Do you have trouble sleeping?'

'I sleep fine.'

'You know, sometimes depression can stop you enjoying things you used to enjoy. We've all been through a lot – and you've seen me experience it myself. It can even dull your senses—'

'I'm not depressed.'

My senses aren't dulled. Quite the opposite.

As if on cue, here it comes. An ominous tingling, like static crackling over my skin, a sensation of momentary weightlessness, a pop in my ears, the colours of the room around me fading, turning sepia, and *BOOM*, the cacophony at the edges of the world comes rushing in.

The high-pitched whine of a scanner at the other end of the building. A pencil scratching on paper at the desk outside. A toddler crying in the waiting room, birds chattering outside the window, a whispered conversation in the corridor.

Then my attention is dragged back into the room.

Lucas has left a trace of lavender soap just under his ear, must have missed it when he was washing this morning. The warmth of his skin helps lift the scent into the air. His perspiration underneath has notes of cumin, chilli and turmeric from last night's dinner, and other things that I know from biology lessons must be electrolytes, pheromones, bacteria, even tiny, harmless amounts of toxins. My brain lays them all out separately for me without my asking or wanting, like an overenthusiastic waiter brandishing a restaurant menu in my face.

Another intrusive thought slides in: his carotid artery is right there, too. For some reason, I know exactly where a bite would sever it. And what would happen next.

Nausea rises, acid in my throat.

I drag my eyes off Lucas's neck, take another sip of water and swallow, trying to get rid of the taste. It eases my throat a little, but it doesn't wash the sensations away. I've been getting them for a while now. When I'm Turned, at least it feels more appropriate; and I can run it off, go sniff things, till it fades. These occasional leaks into my human life are ... unsettling.

My heartbeat quickens and I have to fight to stay calm, reason with myself. It's not like I want to ... you know, actually hurt him. Break his skin with my teeth. The idea is repulsive.

All the same, I need to get a grip on myself.

Finally, the sounds fade away, and the room stops smelling like a cross between an abattoir and a perfume factory. I blink as the colours dial up again, brighter, saturated, normal. *Breathe, Sel. It's over.*

'I think we should talk about the effects of that bite.'

Just as my muscles have started to relax, an electric pulse jolts through my body. He *knows*?

'What ... do you mean?' I croak.

'Emotionally,' he adds, and I breathe again. 'Do you want to talk through that night again? It's clearly still affecting you.'

That night. Our shorthand for twelve hours of horror. The chaotic darkness of the Revenant – marauding, mind-controlling, power-hungry monster, and part-time pensioner. My ex-friend, Harold. He drank Ingrid's blood

5

and mine before he died, and that's why we're now where we are.

Extra. Like *corpus pilori* but with added nuts. I'm picturing a twirling strand of DNA that he broke, or twisted, or grew, but really I have no idea.

'I've already told you everything that happened that night,' I say, picking my words carefully. I *have* been open with him about those hours. Just not about everything since. 'There's no point saying it again. I talk about this stuff all the time with my friends.'

A muscle in his jaw twitches, but he nods, glances down at his notes. 'All right. I'm glad you have friends to confide in, even if you won't talk to me. I know Elena's there for you. We'll move on.'

Elena. His daughter, and my best friend. We've been through everything together. Unlike Mum – who would just go out of her mind with worry – my closest friends now know about mine and Ingrid's current problems. Elena, Pedro, Mika and Ben. Early on, Ingrid told them all what's up.

I haven't told them everything, though. Especially not about what nearly happened with Eddie, my dog. Elena would be shocked. She'd look at me differently. They all would.

I take another slow, calming sip from my glass.

'One strange thing, though: your mum says you tried to rehome your dog with Mika.'

6

The water goes down the wrong way, making me splutter and cough.

Oh, now we're getting too close.

I make the coughing fit last longer than necessary, hoping he'll move on, but he just waits. It's probably one of the techniques he learned in his counselling course.

If I was going to confide in Lucas, this would be the moment. But I know what happens next in these situations: tests. Needles. Isolation, probably. And I've had enough of that to last me a lifetime. Been there, done that, got the T-shirt. Literally – it says *Sequest: Making You Better!* and I've had it for years. I've grown out of it now, but I keep it as a reminder of what they did.

Sequest itself is gone after being exposed for keeping Rippers locked away from the rest of the world. It's been broken up, all its property and tech parcelled out to different companies. One of those, Probius, is a few hours' drive from Tremorglade. It specializes in virus research and has apparently made a breakthrough in the search for a cure for *corpus pilori*. Its biggest cheerleader is Sherman Goss – my chief local hater, head of the Immutable Alliance … and my friend Ben's dad. He's organized a crowdfunder for Probius, to help speed up the process of finding a cure. Maybe they're good people. Maybe they're not. You can bet I won't be mentioning my current situation to them, though. They're not getting their rubber-gloved hands on me.

My leg starts jiggling. 'Uh. What?'

'*Sel.*' He sighs. 'Your dog. Why did you try to give him away?'

'I don't know.'

What else can I say? *I was scared I might eat him?*

This was back when my symptoms first showed up six months ago – I started getting this sudden urge to chase him. Not just the normal play-chasing that Rippers often do. It felt real. Like, if I caught him, I might actually … you know. It took me by surprise, and I panicked. But I'm handling it now. I've found an outlet for those urges when they come: I turn my attention to creatures that I know are fast and agile enough to get away. It's working. I haven't caught anything. Poor Eddie with his little legs might not have made it.

I'm glad I didn't give him away. Luckily Mika's parents said no.

Lucas sits back with a sigh, defeated. Checks his watch. 'We'll leave it there for this week.'

I stand up, energized by relief at making it through the session. 'Thanks. This is, uh, definitely helping.'

He gives me side-eye. We both know it isn't. 'It won't help until you trust me. But that's up to you.'

Trust. Yeah, it's fair to say I have trust issues. You would too, in my position.

As if reading my mind, when I open the door to leave he says, 'We all bear the scars of what Sequest did, Sel.'

Some more than others, though, right?

Are Ingrid and I alone? We weren't the only ones Harold bit. Some of those others died, from blood loss due to his excessive feeding. But a lot of people left Tremorglade in a hurry after dawn came, and in the chaos no one knows how many, if any, of those were his victims too. I've looked around online, but haven't found anyone talking about it. It's something I wonder about.

Our physical wounds are healing. But those bites have left behind more than just scars.

And the scariest thing?

Sometimes, I like it.

CHAPTER 2

Sunday 13 January – HOWL NIGHT

Sergeant Hale has got his head stuck in a bin again.

He's blundering up and down trying to shake it off, crashing into the barriers around the building work at Shady Oaks, barrelling into other Rippers, who assume he's trying to play, and bounce him back. A group of kids are following him, filming him on their phones. They'll edit it along with some music and comedy sound effects later, and pass it around.

Someone snitched and so now he knows why his breath always smells of rotting garbage when he Returns, but it hasn't made any difference. Despite the fact he now eats a huge dinner before dusk on Howl nights in order to prevent it, there's something about foraging for scraps that he can't seem to resist once he has his fur coat on. His nickname these days is Sergeant Trash.

I've no idea why he finds it so appealing. It's not like

I can ask him – only Ingrid and I can understand each other on Howl nights. With every other Ripper, I can get across crude messages like 'go away' and 'let's play', but anything more sophisticated just results in a kind of confused canine 'Ruh?'

My friends who remain human are even more hopeless at understanding anything I say. It's frustrating.

We watch from the riverbank, where we're relaxing together on the wide strip of grass. Eddie sniffs around happily. Mika begged me to let him out to join us – she loved the idea he could be hers and was gutted when her parents said no. I've felt kind of bad I got her hopes up, even if I'm glad he stayed with me in the end.

Right now I'm in a pretty positive mood, no urges more sinister than the usual one to pee up the nearby lamppost. When a squirrel suddenly breaks cover and runs up the fence, I watch it but don't even bother to get up. This is how it is – unpredictable. I'm desperate to find some logic or pattern in my behaviour. Maybe it's because I'm with my friends. Maybe it's going away. Maybe next month I'll go back to losing my mind when I Rip out, like everyone else.

The thought gives me a pang that surprises me: *I hope not.*

I could do without some of the *extra* effects, but being present right now, in this incredible body … I love it. Ripper senses may have leaked into my everyday human life but I don't fully inhabit them until Howl nights. To my disappointment, I haven't yet grown noticeably stronger or faster as a human. If I could have picked, I'd have chosen being good at gym over being able to tell what's in someone else's packed lunch from the other side of the canteen.

Alongside me there's Elena – still not Turning yet, but it surely can't be long now that she's fifteen like me. Her plump cheeks, dimples and sharp, shining eyes make her look like she's constantly on the verge of laughter. Her brother Pedro, now twenty-one, has been Turning for years, but he's bounded off obliviously elsewhere, following a scent. Ben's here – he's fourteen but Immutable like his dad, Sherman, so he'll never Rip out. And Mika is still way too young at twelve, though she's keeping an eye out for the signs: a sudden desire to keep checking out the moon, odd temperature spikes, that sort of thing.

I'm going to miss Mika. Tomorrow, her family are moving out to Greenvale, the brand-new town that's being built up north. Her parents are builders and there's loads of work there. According to Mika, the idea is that it will be a community designed to be inclusive – Turners and Immutables alike. Anyone that moves there will have to sign up to a commitment to peaceful coexistence.

I can see the appeal of starting again somewhere with a blank page. Tremorglade has so much history that it feels like there's no room to write a new chapter. People just keep arguing about what's already happened, what it means, and whose fault it is.

My friends are all wrapped up in their big winter coats against the cold. I have mine on too, natural and far better quality than theirs – thick, fluffy-soft undercoat and a coarser, waterproof top layer. Keeps me cool on warm nights, and warm on cool ones.

They're all laughing their heads off at Hale's antics, and I join in, except my laughter comes out as a series of weird little yips that makes them turn to me in concern.

'Is Sel okay?!' Ben asks, moonlight glinting off his close-cropped, stiff black curls. He leans over and ruffles my neck fur. He's not supposed to hang out with any of us, but his dad is doing something with his dodgy Immutable friends tonight so will be none the wiser. 'It sounds like he's in pain.'

'Check his paws,' says Elena. 'Maybe he got a thorn or something.'

To my surprise, Mika pipes up, 'He's laughing! Can't you tell?' Eddie is lying contentedly in her lap, getting constant strokes.

Ben looks sceptical. 'Not really. I keep forgetting he's still himself in there. Sorry, that *you're* still yourself,' he says awkwardly, turning to me briefly. My friends try to include me, but since I can't reply, they naturally fall into talking about me in the third person, like I'm not there at all. 'I don't suppose normal Rippers have a sense of humour, do they?'

'Don't see why not,' Mika retorts. 'Elephants do. I read

13

about it.' She sits up and efficiently re-does her dark, silky-straight ponytail, pulling it tight behind her head with both hands. Eddie's head pops up in dismay and nudges her elbow, demanding her full attention back on stroking. 'And so do dogs, don't they, Eddie?'

Mika giggles and gathers him up higher into her arms, pushes her nose into his soft fur and kisses his head. He doesn't even struggle away from her. He's a little more wary of me, now. He still comes for a cuddle sometimes, but if I move too fast or take him by surprise, he flinches away.

He hasn't quite forgiven me yet.

As my friends get back to chatting amongst themselves, suddenly I feel horribly lonely. Separate.

If I don't have them, who else do I have?

Ingrid jokes about my online *fans*, but I'm not so stupid as to think they're the same as friends. Besides, if you have fans, you have haters, too.

Things are tense right now. The surviving members of Sherman's Alliance mostly scattered after what happened with the Revenant, but he's recently somehow recruited a whole lot more into Tremorglade. These ones seem even more fanatical about the Immutable cause. They tend to walk around in pairs wearing camo gear, and those trousers that have loads of pockets. Plus, they're armed. Some of them wear balaclavas – the friendliest and most innocent of accessories. Apparently, Sherman put out a call for volunteers to form a 'Tremorglade taskforce', on the private section of his website, the bit you have to pay to subscribe to. What's the 'task' in taskforce? Good question. No one seems to know.

We fall silent as a couple of the Alliance walk by, drinking from soda cans, in their camo uniform. Being newbies, they don't always recognize me and my friends, but when they do, they often try to make trouble for us. Just now they don't notice us – their attention is on Hale. They film him on their phones, with looks of disgust, and I feel a weird surge of outrage on his behalf. *We're* allowed to make fun of him, not them. We just tease, they really despise. As we watch, one of them drops his empty can, kicks it, and then scolds the nearest kid for littering. On Howl nights, they act like they own this town. They stroll around like they're police on patrol, even though no one's given them any authority. Mayor Warren can't seem to do anything about it.

None of the regional authorities want much to do with Tremorglade, these days. It didn't even officially exist until recently, and no one wants to take responsibility for us. Hastaville, our closest town, has drawn its boundaries up to the edge of the forest, where the wall used to be, and is reluctant to interfere across the line.

And it's not just Tremorglade that's tense. The whole Ripper thing is still so new to everyone beyond our town, and there are plenty of people all around the world reacting badly. A lot of places are struggling to maintain order.

Something darker has replaced the unrest of the early days following the Rippocalypse. Conspiracy theories – about Sequest, about me, about Tremorglade, and a million different ideas about what causes Turning. In some places, especially out in the countryside, mobs have uprooted the phone masts, convinced the virus travels via the signals. In the cities, gangs have taken to raiding pharmaceutical companies, smashing everything, claiming that they're poisoning us into Turning. And there's a common thread in a lot of these conspiracy theories. Online, the same memes.

My face.

Occasionally Ingrid's. Pedro's and Elena's too. But mainly mine. I'm the only one who was daft enough to put myself on video, to make millions of strangers feel like they know me. When the rest of the world started becoming Rippers, I wanted to reassure people, to explain what to expect, to help them adjust. And I really did help a lot of viewers – I get messages every day telling me so. But I get other messages too. Not so nice ones.

Imagine if *those* people found out what I've been up to lately.

I give myself a shake, and decide to go find Ingrid. I know where she'll be – on her own in the forest somewhere nearby.

It's still early in the evening, and the air is full of a thousand different animal sounds and intriguing scents that call to me. I get up, stretch, and lollop away, conscious of their eyes on my back. I look good, I know it. Streamlined, elegant, fluid. Couldn't be more different from human Sel – when human Sel runs, PE teachers shake their heads despairingly.

The process of Turning is a hot mess, and seeing yourself do it is even grosser. Organs and skin bubbling and popping, a beast inside you that's been cooped up for too long, fighting to get out. It's not painful, just … alarming.

Returning, though, couldn't be more different. Blurry, slow, each hair softening like butter on my arms, thinning and growing more transparent and insubstantial, as though the fur is melting away. My claws shrink back gently, sculpting into my chewed fingernails. My muscles relax. It's a little sad, like saying goodbye to a good friend.

Tonight, that farewell is hours away yet.

Ingrid's waiting for me a little way along the path. Her fur in the moonlight is the richest red-brown along her spine. Her scent reaches me and I breathe it in, mixed with pine: a unique perfume that calms me when I'm near her. There's a trace of her human self in it – slightly sweet, slightly sharp – just as there's always a trace of Ripper when she's human.

Her voice arrives in my head as I join her. 'Hey.' We can

talk when we're close enough – a kind of communication signal gets passed, I guess. Don't ask me how it works; I'm not a scientist. Probably body language, smells, sounds, whatever. But I love it. It's intimate.

She sniffs me. 'Oh, Ben's out tonight? Glad he managed to get away from his dad.'

My friends have left fresh traces of themselves on me. Ingrid's nostrils can identify all of them in an instant, as if they've signed my T-shirt.

'I was just thinking, do you reckon we'll start getting Ripper strength and speed as humans?' I ask. 'That would be sick, don't you think?'

The look she turns on me is properly disgusted. 'Being less human, you mean?'

'No, that's not what I—'

'Are you *glad* you got bitten?'

I'm stunned. Where did *that* come from? 'Of course not! I'm just saying it's not *all* bad.' From her expression, I'm making it worse. 'You said yourself, we have to stay positive. That's all I'm—'

She stiffens and starts sniffing the air. 'Shh.'

Then I smell the same thing she does: a bear.

When the wall came down, a few moved into our forest. Their existence makes some people nervous, but I don't mind them. I much prefer having them around than the Immutable Alliance lot. The bears usually keep a respectful distance.

This one's a female. She senses us around the same time we spot her, and freezes. It's a smart thing to do, as my eyesight comes into its own in the dark, and it's attuned to movements.

We all stand there for a few seconds, just taking each other in.

She's massive. Not prey for a Ripper, by any stretch of the imagination.

All the same, for a moment, there's the faintest impulse, a flare of excitement in my belly. A sly suggestion: *Wouldn't it feel good to chase her?* Maybe I'd even catch her. I reckon we'd be fairly evenly matched.

My rational brain kicks in: *why* would I do that?

I consciously relax my muscles. See? I have self-control.

The bear finally shifts, turning away slowly and walking on all fours carefully through the trees, looking back once to check if we're following.

I'm about to carry on my argument with Ingrid when another scent invades my nostrils, coming from just ahead of us. A far worse one.

Sherman.

It takes me a few seconds to spot Ben's dad in the darkness, but then there's a glint of something metal next to a tree trunk – the barrel of a gun. It follows the path of the bear. He's going to shoot her.

Ingrid and I start barking at the same time, the sounds slicing through the night a fraction of a second before the gunshot. The bear takes off, veering away from Sherman and crashing through the woods.

Sherman's head pops round the tree trunk and he sees us. For a terrifying second I think he's going to take aim at me and Ingrid, but then he swears and makes off after the bear.

'What is he *thinking*?' I say, but Ingrid isn't listening. Her brow crinkles, the reddish hairs bunching together.

'The bear's headed towards town.'

With a sinking feeling, I realize Ingrid's right. The terrified bear is galloping right into Tremorglade.

We overtake Sherman within seconds, his heavy boots and awkward, clumsy movements making him seem weighed down with rocks compared to us. My limbs are fluid and every muscle in balance as I leap bracken and stumps, effortlessly adjusting in the air to land sure-footed on flexible pads before launching off again.

Ingrid moves ahead, neck stretched forward, focused. I ask my body for more and it responds smoothly, like an engine shifting up a gear.

Moonlight floods us as we break the treeline and thunder over the little wooden bridge, the river flowing fast beneath. There are my friends, still sitting on the grass a hundred metres or so away. Their slow ears, eyes and noses are oblivious to the bear galloping towards them.

Eddie sees her, though, and lets off a volley of yaps,

leaping to his feet and jumping up and down, his little body vibrating with alarm.

I can smell the bear's fear. All she knows is that she's under attack, and she will try to survive the only way she knows how, destroying anyone who gets in her way.

Finally they all see her, their instincts so horribly slow. Elena's eyes widen and her arm reaches out for Mika, who stops mid-chatter with Ben. Clambering awkwardly to their grass-stained knees, they don't stand a chance. The bear's going to kill them.

CHAPTER 3

There's a couple of seconds still between me and the bear. Now my friends are all on their feet, scattering in panic, but she's almost on top of them.

Eddie, snarling his head off, bounds onto the creature's huge furry back.

I'm a few paces behind Ingrid as she shoots past the bear, overtaking then twisting round in front, braking, her skidding claws raking furrows through the grass just in front of our friends. The bear slows, unsure, half-turning to deal with Eddie on her back. That's all the invitation I need. A fraction of a second later I leap, swiping Eddie away as I land. With a yelp, his body flies off onto the grass, but he's straight back up on his feet again, yapping from a safe distance.

The bear and I go down together in a growling, snarling frenzy of fangs and claws, snapping jaws and flying fur. I sink my teeth into the closest part of her body, which turns out to be her hind leg. I apply pressure, feeling the resistance of the bone. Her roar travels through my head and shakes my frame but I don't let go, tugging from side to side. Her blood flows across my tongue. Fighting back, she whips her head round and goes for my shoulder, connecting through fur and breaking skin, but she's not as strong as I am – she's weakened by my attack. I barely register the pain, overcome with a need to give everything, to protect my pack. Right now, I don't care if I die. I won't stop until she can't hurt anyone.

The world seems to slow down, flowing thick and viscous like treacle. Somewhere, faintly, I can hear Ingrid barking incessantly, but it loses its meaning. As I subdue the bear everything else fades away leaving nothing but me and my prey. I marvel at the strength of my body, glory in it, bathe in it, luxuriate. Everything I ask for, it gives me. Precision, strength, skill. The blood is singing through my veins. I have control, power. I've never felt like this. Not even close.

'Sel! Stop! Stop! That's enough!'

There's a shocked note in Ingrid's voice that filters through to my brain and makes me loosen my grip on the now unresisting bear. The narrow focus of my vision expands again to take in my immediate surroundings.

Mika and Elena are standing just the other side of Ingrid, clutching each other, Mika in tears but apparently unharmed. I don't see Ben, so he must have got away.

We did it. We saved them. *I* did.

I blink, my head a little hazy. Ingrid slinks over, sniffs at the bear's leg wound and listens to its heartbeat. I can hear it even from here – fast and fluttery.

'She's really hurt. She'd already stopped, Sel, you didn't need to ...' Ingrid turns, my eyes meet hers, and a prickling of doubt runs through me.

'Maybe ... one of the Immutables at the ... Wellness Centre can ...' My voice sounds slurred, almost drunk.

A shadow passes over me, the barrel of a rifle, and a shot rings out. My body jolts, and for half a moment I think it's me who's been shot. Then Ingrid. But it's neither of us.

The bear has gone utterly still.

Sherman lowers the gun, breathing hard.

There's a glacial silence for a few moments. The kids who were filming Sergeant Hale earlier slowly stand up from their hiding places behind a garden fence. Hale himself is nowhere to be seen.

No one seems to know what to do. Sherman just stands there, holding the rifle ready, as if maybe he hasn't finished with it yet. Several other Alliance people have arrived, too, forming a wide semicircle around us, looking to Sherman like they're waiting for permission.

Eddie's sudden frantic yapping makes us all turn towards the river. He's bouncing up and down on the bank, barking.

There's something in the moonlit water. A shape, half submerged. A human shape.

Ben. He must have jumped in to get away from the bear. The way he's bobbing up and down with the water flow, face down, tells me he's unconscious. His coat has ballooned on top, his head bowed under the surface.

'*Ben!*' Sherman starts running towards him.

The waterfall is not far downstream. We lost Pedro over it, once.

Not happening again on my watch.

I pass Sherman within moments, still throbbing with adrenaline from my encounter with the bear, and leap right over Eddie, plunging into the water. In my haste I land almost on top of Ben and he's pushed further under the surface. Momentarily blinded, I grab for him. My jaws close around fur, and for a second I think he's somehow lost his Immutability, that he Turned when he entered the water, but the texture is wrong, the fur is fake – it's the lining of his hood. I have it in my teeth and start swimming him to the bank, my powerful legs pushing the water aside like paddles. Ahead of us I see Ingrid on the grass, ready to jump in if I lose him. Sherman reaches the edge and leaps in, flailing around, trying to stay afloat, buffeted by the current. Never mind him.

The hood starts to tear away from the coat, my fangs severing the stitches. I quickly transfer my grip to Ben's wrist and power us the rest of the way, dragging him up the bank, sopping and heavy.

Elena and Mika take hold of him and turn him over,

checking his airway, starting CPR, till water gushes out of his mouth and he explodes into coughs.

Through my relief, I'm only barely conscious of Sherman arriving next to us, dripping, his boots sloshing water over the rims. I didn't even realize he'd made it out. He staggers over, kneels next to Ben as he starts to sit up, grasping him by the shoulders and clutching him to his chest, sobbing. 'I thought I'd lost you.' I've never seen him show any emotion other than anger. I didn't know he was even capable of it.

'Sel saved him,' Mika says. She's cradling Eddie in her arms like he's a baby, and he just lies there, gazing up at her solemnly as if reminding her that he played his part, too.

I did save Ben. I really did.

Sherman glances at me, his wet olive skin gleaming, muscles straining against his jacket. Seeing the two of them together, it strikes me again how little Ben looks like his dad. He's so small and slight in Sherman's huge arms, it seems like one tiny movement could crush him.

Sherman looks utterly confused, and I know why. To him, I've always been the big bad wolf. Well, the bad wolf, anyway. And yet here I am, the reason his son is still breathing. Of course it doesn't make sense to him – his world has been built entirely on lies, starting from when Harold began to radicalize him online, before he ever came to Tremorglade. When the Revenant appeared, dragging Rippers away on Howl night and biting them, Sherman blamed us, and right up to this day he refuses to believe the Revenant was actually Harold. He still thinks I had something to do with the whole episode, that I was behind it, even.

He's never been able to see the truth.

Do I dare hope that now, finally, he'll figure it out?

CHAPTER 4

Ingrid

My room at Juniper House has a good view of the rainy street below. I'm nervous, waiting for Sel to arrive. I sit on the windowsill listening to the radio news, watching for him to appear. We often meet up here with the others after school – for a children's home, this place is actually pretty nice. Amy and Bernice have put a lot of effort into making it cosy. Plus, my room is bigger than Elena's or Sel's, and as for Ben's ... well, none of us is getting invited *there* any time soon, even after Sel's heroics.

I'm going over and over in my mind how I should tell him. I've been worried for a while, but now, I'm actually scared.

The radio isn't helping. The news is full of rioting and

soaring crime. Ripper Cultists clash with Immutables to the south. Before the Rippocalypse we were told the rest of the world was violent and scary, in order to keep us here. Now, it really is. I turn the radio off.

To distract myself, I fiddle a postcard between my fingers – it came this morning, neatly addressed to me here at Juniper House. On the front is a bright red-and-gold text logo – SLAY PR – and a slogan: *Glow Up Your Message!* The stamp is from Pyrum, a county some distance to the north-east, not too far from Greenvale.

'It's your public relations!' Bernice joked when she handed it over earlier. She doesn't really get what a public relations company does, but she did like the guys that own SLAY PR, Jim and Tom. 'How nice of them to keep in touch!'

The two of them visited Tremorglade as tourists, and frankly they couldn't have picked a worse time. They were enthusiastic enough when they arrived – big fans of Sel, of course – and great supporters of Turning, but after the Revenant's biting rampage that night, they packed up and left before Sel and I were even out of hospital. I was half expecting the other side of the postcard to be an invoice for their therapy or something.

But it's just a cheery, very short note.

Ingrid! How ARE you? We miss you! Come visit us in the mountains any time if you would enjoy a change. We're loving it! Their two looping signatures are at the bottom, and a PO Box address.

It's more than a little odd, considering I barely met them. But then, I'm one of the original escapees from Tremorglade, and some people are still star-struck by that. Sel gets most of the fans because of his videos, but I do have a few. If we were a band, I'd be the drummer.

I bend and unbend the card impatiently round my finger while I check the street again. Finally a familiar figure rounds the corner, holding his coat over his head against the rain, and takes the stairs up to Juniper's front door, two at a time. He's jaunty, in a good mood.

After last week, he's the golden boy for some people round here – those who already approved of him. Those who didn't have gone quiet for the moment. Some of the kids recorded most of what happened, from behind the building-site hoarding. A Ripper fighting a bear, then saving a kid? Despite the fact they think he didn't know what he was doing, everyone is giving him the credit anyway, and he's lapping it up. Even Sherman isn't giving him a hard time this week, though he's stopped short of actually thanking him for saving Ben. Sel's been in a spectacularly positive mood ever since. Bernice and Amy love him, but even they've commented that he's milking it.

I sound bitter, don't I? He *is* a hero. No doubt about it. Ben might have drowned if it hadn't been for him. Sel's had a lot of hate, so I can't begrudge him enjoying a bit of love around here, for once.

And we're really close these days. We understand each other in a way no one else can, since we're both *extra pilori* now, our senses picking up on things others don't notice. Not that he was ever that hard to read. Emotions have always flickered over his face like sunlight on water.

But now he really can't hide anything from me.

For example: this good mood of his? The hormonal surge, the proteins and peptides that flooded his body and mingled in his scent – I know when it really started, and it wasn't when he knew Ben was safe.

It was when he chased and brought down the bear.

» » »

Sel comes in, gives me a big grin while handing over a paper bag with one of his mum's chocolate pastries in it, and immediately starts devouring his own, before spotting my postcard.

'Oh, you got one too!' I let him take it and read it, and he laughs. 'I thought it was just me. Thought they'd seen my newfound popularity and wanted in. Use me for an ad campaign or something.' He winks to let me know he's not entirely serious, and takes a huge bite of his pastry. 'So, where's Elena and Ben? You know, we haven't played poker with them for ages but it struck me we could totally destroy them, now. We could tell their bluffs easy, what with our souped-up skills.'

This is exactly the problem. 'I actually wanted to talk

to you ... alone.' I start gently. 'I've been meaning to say something for a while.'

'Yeah?' Sel's skin flushes, his eyes flick to mine, and they look hopeful. A slow smile begins at the edges of his lips.

I know he likes me. Serotonin and oxytocin are practically flooding from his pores.

Best do this quickly, like ripping off a plaster.

'You're letting it take over, aren't you?'

'Mm?' His jaw pauses mid-chew.

'You enjoyed attacking that bear. Tell me you didn't.'

With that, the grin slides from his face. 'What? I was defending our friends. We both were.' He looks slightly ridiculous, talking through an engorged cheek full of food, like a hamster.

It doesn't escape my notice that he avoided answering. 'I was there, Sel. You were ...' I frown, searching for the right word. 'Ecstatic. I smelled it.'

'You *smelled* it.' He swallows, and one side of his mouth quirks up again. 'Well, you know what they say: she who smelt it dealt it, Ing.'

'Don't be such a child.'

'Come on, that's not fair. It was adrenaline – you know, that stuff we need in emergencies, Rippers and humans too. That's how we can run faster, be stronger.' He softens slightly, and a teasing glint comes into his big brown eyes. 'You're exactly the same when you do taekwondo. You should have seen your face after you won the final against Becky last year. When she went down clutching her leg in agony you were totally pumped.'

'That's different. It's sport.' As I say it, it sounds weak, hypocritical. But I plough on. 'And you know that's not the point.'

'So what is the point? Why are you being like this?' He's hurt. The lovey-dovey chemicals have dried up. 'I should have let our friends get attacked?'

I'm handling this badly. What's coming off him now is cortisol – stress, anxiety. Anger. His mouth shuts into a sulky line.

'That's just it. The bear had stopped. I was in front of it. You'd have noticed that, if you hadn't lost your head.' He starts to object but I talk over him. 'Our new instincts are powerful. You can't play around with them. You need to shut them down.'

He takes a step towards me, draws in a breath through his nostrils, testing my scent. His eyebrows pop up in surprise. 'You're scared of me!'

I can't help but laugh. 'I'm really not.'

'I know what fear smells like.' He looks confused. 'You honestly think I'm so out of control I'd hurt you?'

'I don't think that.'

All those extra senses and he still doesn't have a clue. He can smell my fear, but he's wrong about what I'm afraid of. As if *I'd* be scared of *him*.

I'm the one who's an actual murderer.

It doesn't matter that the Revenant was controlling my mind when I killed Arty. It doesn't matter that Arty was a liar, that she didn't care if any of us got hurt, that she was only interested in getting control of the Revenant for her own purposes. It doesn't change the fact that it was my claws and teeth that ended her. I was a spectator of my own Ripper body, a fully immersive experience with all the sounds, sensations, tastes of tearing fangs, screams, blood. Worse, I remember how it felt to revel in that bloodshed. To enjoy it. I never want to feel that way again. When I get a surge of *extra pilori* it's like a door opening, an invitation to step back into that chaos. If Sel is tempted through, I'm scared I'll go with him. It's myself I'm frightened of.

Sel only had a few hours under that beast's control, and he didn't do anything worse than smash a glass door in the Wellness Centre. It's not the same.

That's why I spend all my energy on keeping the door closed against *extra*. I know what I'm capable of.

Sel believes he can leave his door ajar, just a little.

As though reading my thoughts, he says, 'Can you open your mind to the idea that maybe not everything about *extra* is bad? I know it came from something negative, but that doesn't mean the effects are all bad. I did something good with it, saving Ben. If I can learn how to control it on the quiet, use it for good, I can prove to all those haters online that I'm not the evil person they think I am. Once they see that, we can be more open about what's happened to us.'

I shake my head. 'Sel, you don't need to *prove* you're worthy of their respect. You can't make them love you. Especially not by messing about with something so dangerous.'

He curls an arm round my shoulder, gives me a reassuring squeeze. He seems genuinely upset that I might be afraid of him. 'I'd never hurt you, or anyone. Ever. Come on, you know me.' His face is pleading. 'I promise I'm not messing around with it. It's the opposite – I'm learning. The more I learn, the more control I'll have.' He's so obviously desperate not to have a fight that I don't have the heart to keep going. I've said my piece.

I slip gently out from under his arm, move to the window. Outside, the day is still dull and drizzly, the street empty.

'You're still going to visit Probius, right?' I ask.

'I said I would, didn't I?' His words are muffled by another mouthful of pastry.

He's not happy about it, but I think it's a good idea. Those of us who originally escaped from Tremorglade have had an invitation to visit the lab, meet the research team working on *corpus pilori*. They say they want to be open and transparent about what they're doing, show us that they're no Sequest.

We're going separately – Sel with his mum in ten days' time, on Wednesday, me with Bernice on Thursday, Elena and Pedro on Friday, so that we all get individual attention and a chance to ask questions in private. Sel's made me promise not to let slip to them anything about the changes he and I are experiencing. He's wary. He acts as though all scientists are evil, all companies like Sequest.

Sherman being a supporter of Probius does *not* help. I must admit, I feel kind of icky having anything in common with the guy. But if Sel's so keen to squash some of the rumours about him, surely the first step would be showing people he's not against the whole idea of a cure being available for those who want it.

Sherman has his own channel, like Sel used to, and that's where a lot of those rumours started life. It's an online community of like-minded people, which goes by the name of Facts Unleashed. Immutable Alliance, mainly, but plenty of disgruntled Turners as well. There are people posting rebuttals to Sel's old videos, explaining why they're all lies – and a forum.

On the forum, people across the world discuss our failings in great detail – mine, Sel's, Elena's and Pedro's – with zero knowledge about us or about what really happened in the lead-up to the Rippocalypse and beyond. Conspiracy theories appear on there every day, mutating and evolving whenever people whose profiles are random strings of numbers add their thoughts. They have reams of so-called 'data' to prove their ideas. Sel gets the worst of it, because his face is the most visible. Some of them think he's behind every bad thing that ever happens; others say he's basically a puppet controlled by outside forces.

I glance behind me, watch him licking his fingers. There's a big dollop of chocolate on his chin which he goes to wipe off but instead it drops onto his jeans. If he is being controlled by outside forces, they don't have very good coordination.

Sighing, I twist back to the window. A few people are trudging along in waterproofs out there, heads down. They all look the same from up here. You can't tell who's on which side. It didn't feel like there even were 'sides' not so long ago. People had individual arguments with each other, of course – who doesn't? – but lately it's felt different. Like the whole community is pulling apart into two groups. Pro Turning and Anti Turning. Pro Sel and Anti Sel. Obviously I'm Pro Sel, but the other one's … complicated.

Behind me Sel shifts and his silence feels ominous. Eventually he says, carefully casual, 'So, this cure, then, if they ever make it work … you wouldn't actually consider … might you take it, then? Even if it stopped you Turning at all?'

'In a heartbeat.'

I was fine with Ripping out, for the few months I had of doing it the normal way. If it was still like that – if I checked out for Howl nights like everyone else, and woke up happy, if I didn't get intrusive Ripper sensations in the middle of Geography – there'd be no problem. The Revenant ruined everything. Now I just want out.

I haven't told Sel, but last Howl night, after the bear incident, I went home feeling deflated and sad. And I don't know how I did it, but I Returned to human for a few seconds. Literally just a few seconds, before I pinged back. Afterwards, I felt like I'd run a marathon, but I did it. It's given me hope. Next Howl night, I'm going to try it again. While Sel tries to spend more time as a Ripper, I'm practising being human.

The rain is coming down harder, the paving slabs a shiny blur.

I don't need to look round to know Sel's sensed what I'm thinking. His crushing disappointment is heavy in the air.

CHAPTER 5

Sel

Wednesday 30 January

My uneasy stomach starts properly rolling the moment the taxi's tyres crunch up the private road to the lab. Mum and I have been driven through narrow countryside lanes for twenty minutes with only the odd farmhouse and smattering of sheep in sight, when the road takes a sharp turn through trees and opens out to reveal the Probius building.

It's a fair size. A few storeys, a nondescript grey concrete box with windows all round. It looks somehow military, an impression strengthened by the ten-foot razor-wire fence all round it. When we reach the gatehouse, a friendly, efficient guard asks us to get out and takes us through security checks, scanning our bodies and bags. Our cab driver turns back down the road, having told us to call when we're ready to leave.

The security guard phones someone to tell them we're here, then turns to us. 'Wait here – the prof won't be long.' Then he frowns at me. 'You all right?'

I nod and turn aside, not bothering to hide my foul mood.

'We're very pleased to be here,' Mum says, giving me a warning glare.

I stick my hands in my pockets. I just want this to be over.

Ingrid wants to stop Turning completely, and I can't get my head around it. I get that being *extra* comes with challenges, and it was scary at first, but the more I think about it, the more I realize it's a privilege to be able to experience full moon nights as Rippers. Plus, it's given us a special bond, and I thought that meant something to her. Instead, she can't wait to throw it away.

I'm not going to ask these guys anything about the cure. She can ask them herself tomorrow, if she wants it so much.

The prof turns out to be a bald, pink-faced man who shakes Mum's hand and tries to greet me with a fist bump, which I look at blankly as though I've never seen knuckles before.

It's hard to tell how old he is but I guess in his fifties. He's wearing jeans and a Federal Agenda T-shirt, with a glimpse of tattoo at the neck. Mum looks dubious.

'Professor Wilcox?' Her tone distinctly says, *Are you sure?*

'That's me. But call me Gerry.' He smiles warmly at

me. 'I'm really glad you're here, Sel. I totally understand if you're nervous about today, but I promise you nothing bad will happen. You deserve to know exactly what we're about. Nothing is off limits. Ask any questions, and I'll answer honestly. Okay?'

'Thank you, we will,' Mum says.

I shrug.

» » »

Gerry takes us on a tour, showing us various boring labs and offices, introducing us to his team, whose names I instantly forget. Some labs are only small, but a couple are as big as our hall at school.

There's a lot that doesn't seem related to *corpus pilori*. A couple of the smaller rooms look like little more than storage areas, stacked high with equipment. Gerry explains that they inherited a lot of stuff from Sequest that they're not currently using. Abandoned research projects they'll get to eventually but are not a priority. He shows us a huge freezer behind a passcoded door, full of endless rows of samples. He starts telling us about a few of them. I fail to stifle a huge yawn.

'Well, I sense we should move on to the main event.' He winks at me, and we move back out to the corridor.

'We've a way to go yet, but we're much closer to finding a cure, now.' He sounds excited, and looks at me expectantly, like I'm going to be delighted.

I decide to lay my cards on the table. 'I'm not interested in a cure, for myself.'

I expect him to be taken aback, but he doesn't seem to be in the slightest. He nods. 'Me neither.'

I blink at him. 'Huh?'

'You're surprised. I can understand that. But I have no problems Turning, personally. Our aim is not to eradicate *corpus pilori*, despite what some pressure groups want. Ripping out has improved my physical and mental health in myriad ways. There is ample evidence that it has many positive effects on the human part of our lives. So no, I don't want to lose that. But I know others who do, desperately. Turning is not for everyone.'

Ingrid's face swims into my mind. *In a heartbeat.* That's what she said. Mum looks perky at the thought, too. She's never exactly embraced Howl nights.

'My work is for those people. And to arm those of us who *do* want to Turn with knowledge about our own condition. We assume it's stable, but we don't know for sure. It could evolve, change. In fact, that's what we're mainly looking for – minuscule changes in the virus, that would unlock our understanding of how it works.'

Minuscule changes? I think to myself. *If only you knew.*

'The more we understand it, the closer we are to everyone being able to live happily with or without it.'

I don't know what to say. 'Oh.'

Gerry wants to know if I have any questions, but the

only ones I can think of are ones I'm not ready to ask. Mum has plenty. She asks him pointedly about how Probius is different from Sequest, what kinds of safeguards they have in place to stop them turning evil – okay, she doesn't put it quite like that, but it's what she means. She wants to know if he understands how his work is being pounced on by people like Sherman, and how it's being used to stir up divisions.

'Oh yes,' Gerry says. 'Our team is very aware of Sherman Goss. He has his own agenda, and it has little to do with ours. All we can do is keep on with our research, and publicly counter any false statements he comes up with. This is why you're here, and why we'll be inviting the media in more. Openness and transparency are how we win hearts and minds, I really believe that. Handled in the right way, our work should heal divisions, not cause them.'

Mum seems slightly reassured. I still don't know what to think.

Gerry takes us through a door to some stairs. 'Let me show you our most exciting project.'

On the next floor we stop and Gerry makes us rub gel on our hands and don lab coats before taking us down a corridor past closed doors with large metallic numbers on. At the end, next to a fire exit, there's one labelled 909.

With a flourish, he touches his card to the reader and the door clicks open. The space is tiny, with a dazzling white floor and walls. The air is much warmer in here, and I can feel the sweat breaking out on my top lip and in my armpits. A clear glass tank rests on a low stand, about a metre across and a metre high, covered with a thick metal lid. A tall, bald man is standing next to it, staring intently through the glass with a frown. His lab coat hangs open to reveal a loud plaid shirt underneath. He practically jumps out of his skin when we open the door.

'Oh, sorry,' Gerry says. 'I hope we're not interrupting. I thought your shift was over.'

The guy laughs. 'It is. I'm just checking on our guest.' He speaks with a soft western burr. 'I got a temperature alert just as I was headed out, but as far as I can tell that seems to have been an error. She's fine. Help yourself.' He steps back so we can see the tank better.

I peer into the tank. There's some gravel and a couple of rocks in it, but no water. Other than that, it's empty.

'Meet our breakthrough,' says Gerry, proudly. 'Her scientific name is *barbaesis veloptera*, so we call her Barb. She's actually hermaphroditic – male *and* female – but more female. Besides, we think the name suits her.' He turns to the guy. 'Owen, we'd like to watch her feed, if you don't mind.'

For half a second, Owen seems annoyed, like he wants to tell us to get lost, but then he shrugs. 'Sure. Any second now. Always hungry, our Barb.'

Gerry explains to us, 'Barb needs to feed very frequently, or she'll die. This tank gives her what she needs automatically. Every few minutes.'

Just then, a clear cylinder slides down into the tank from the lid with an electronic whirr. Sitting at the bottom of it is a red sphere, about the size of a ping-pong ball.

Out of the corner of my eye, I swear I spot something moving down by one of the rocks, but when I look, I don't see anything.

Then, with a puff of air, the red ball drops out of the cylinder.

It doesn't even have time to hit the floor before something long, grey and thin like a shoelace shoots out from behind the rock and wraps around the ball, curling itself round and round until there's no trace of red visible, only the creature's body like a coil of rope.

'Good grief, what is that?' Mum asks faintly.

'Barb is a unique type of parasite,' Gerry says. 'We believe she *might* hold the key to our cure.'

'She does,' Owen says quietly beside me. 'I know it.'

I can't look away. The parasite, wrapped around her dinner, starts to judder violently, thrashing around on the floor of the tank so that the gravel scatters around it. Pinpricks of red spray begin to dot the glass.

'Is that ... blood?' I ask.

'Indeed. Not just any old blood, though.'

She's really going at it, vibrating like a pneumatic drill. A red mist begins to form in the air around her.

Within seconds, it's over. The creature unfurls, much more slowly than before. There's nothing left of her meal.

She begins moving, thin body undulating, around the bottom of the tank, cleaning up methodically, scouring each pebble in turn. She scootches across the glass in front of us, cleaning up the sprayed droplets through little openings in her slug-like skin.

We're mesmerized. The glass squeaks quietly as she moves across it, her hundreds of tiny mouths sucking at it.

'Gorgeous, isn't she?' Owen breathes, right next to me.

It's not exactly the first word that sprang to mind, but I must admit, she is impressive. Nothing is left, and the glass sparkles again.

After a moment, Gerry appears to remember what we're here for.

'So, let me explain. When the Tremorglade experiment was in its early days, Sequest drained a lake out in a remote part of the Quartile Peninsula, in order to build on it. They discovered a single, unique creature in the earth underneath it – Barb. She appeared dead, but having brought her in for study, they were amazed to discover that she was alive. She'd been hibernating, who knows for how long. But she was weak. They tried all sorts of things to perk her up, and pretty soon, they discovered that she had a voracious appetite for *corpus pilori*. When they fed her human blood infected with the virus, she grew stronger by the minute. Of course, being Sequest, they didn't just feed it to her like this. They allowed her to feed directly from victims.'

Mum gasps. 'You're not serious?'

I don't know why she's so shocked. It's entirely on brand for Sequest.

'I'm afraid so. Having identified Barb as a parasite, they wanted to see what effect it would have if she attached herself to a human being whose blood contained *corpus pilori*. They picked someone from Tremorglade for the purpose. A woman called Annie Wilson.'

I've never heard of her, but Mum gasps again. 'Annie! She worked in IT. She went on a work trip ... we were told she died in a helicopter accident ...'

Gerry casts his eyes down. None of us says anything for a moment. I'm guessing Annie figured out something that Sequest didn't want her to know, and they decided to make her useful instead of just getting rid of her.

'I'm sorry.' Gerry bites his lip. 'It's awful. But it's important you know the truth.'

Mum and I both jump as the feeding tube pumps out another ball of blood for Barb, and watch, half fascinated, half horrified, as she attacks it once again.

Gerry goes on to say that once Barb attached herself to Annie, she stayed put, and started to feed on her blood. Then something amazing happened. Annie didn't Turn on the next full moon. Barb was eating the *corpus pilori* faster than the virus could replicate.

I stare at the sluggish creature, now luxuriating on the bottom of the tank immediately following her feed. The little sucking mouths along her length open and close in waves, like they're talking to each other. 'So ...' I start.

'She was cured,' Owen finishes for me. 'Never Ripped out again.'

'Except there was one problem,' Gerry sighs. 'Annie started to get sick. Sequest couldn't figure out why. So they scanned her. That's when they saw the problem.'

'Problem?' I ask.

'In the process of feeding on *corpus pilori*, Barb had caused changes inside her host. Annie's entire body was suffering from necrosis, though there was some original brain function left.'

'Necrosis?'

Owen turns to me with an odd look. 'Her organs were rotting away inside her. She was basically a zombie. The living dead. That's what happens if you don't handle Barb carefully enough.'

Acid rises into my throat, and my stomach clenches. Owen's face remains impassive, but there's a glint of something hostile in his eye, like he's enjoying my discomfort.

Gerry shifts uncomfortably. 'Of course, there are no such things as zombies. Owen just means she became very ill. Sel is a *child*, Owen, let's not give him nightmares! Ha ha.'

Rebuked, Owen shrugs and goes back to staring at Barb. Gerry explains, 'In fact, Annie was still able to speak,

48

even making sense, for a while. But her body was being destroyed by a disease you might have heard of. She had an extremely high temperature, combined with skin so cold it turned into frozen flakes.'

'Frozen Fever!' Mum says, hands flying to her mouth. 'Oh, poor Annie.'

I frown. 'I thought Sequest made up Frozen Fever to scare us, to persuade us not to leave Tremorglade. I didn't know it actually existed.'

'Well, they certainly used it to scare you, but it's a real disease. And it nearly became a real problem, out there in the world. They decided to separate Barb from Annie, but security wasn't as tight as it should have been. Before they could carry out the operation, Annie fled. She broke out of Sequest's lab, with Barb still attached to her neck. There were reports of people who'd been in contact with her showing similar symptoms, but even more severe – they weren't just sick, they were irrational, aggressive, incapable of reason.

'Thankfully, the outbreak was quickly handled before it could spread out of control. Sequest pulled out all the stops and managed to round up the victims within a week. Frozen Fever was re-contained back in the lab and the whole incident was hushed up. They removed Barb from Annie and, sadly, Annie died within minutes. So did all the others.'

Owen chimes in, 'All rotted from the inside out. Bodies were mush. Basically, they fell apart.'

Gerry adds quickly, 'So, ever since then, we're left only with Barb once again.'

Mum is looking a little green. I'm not feeling too good myself. Gerry continues.

'Anyway, the point is, if we can only figure out a way to harness her virus-extracting abilities in a *safe* way, without causing Frozen Fever, we'll be on to something.'

Owen looks levelly at Gerry. 'I mean, we do have ideas. If some of us were allowed to explore them.'

'But we're not there yet,' Gerry says firmly, and I can see there's some kind of dispute between them on this subject. 'We have to go slowly. We can't risk mistakes. And we certainly won't risk anyone's health. Don't worry. No one will be touching Barb any time soon, not on my watch. When we need to take samples, we use robotic tongs.' He shows us how a mechanical arm moves around inside the tank.

Gerry senses we've had enough, and we all head out. The air in the corridor is much cooler, which is a relief. Owen gives us a brief nod goodbye before letting himself through another door further down.

As we're shown round the other rooms on this floor, my mind is racing.

The thought of Ingrid not Turning anymore is a gut punch. But Gerry's words have been percolating inside my head. Our *extra pilori* virus is a mutated version of the *corpus pilori* everyone else has. Studying *extra* might be a

50

big help. I wasn't expecting to trust anyone here. Thought I'd learned never to do that. But my instincts tell me Gerry is decent. My judgement about people is a lot better than it used to be, now I can use scent information, and all his signs are genuine. I can't say the same for Owen, but he's not the boss.

And I have to admit, one huge benefit has struck me. Gerry might be able to give us more information about how we're different, me and Ingrid. Like, *extra pilori* doesn't seem to be hugely contagious in the same way that normal *corpus pilori* is, otherwise everyone else would have it by now. Maybe he could tell us more about its potential, the skills it's given us. He might be able to reassure Ingrid, get her to see the positive side.

I don't want to say anything yet. I'll sleep on it, make sure this is really what I want to do. But maybe in the morning I'll give him a call. Tell him in confidence.

My attention is flagging after another half hour, but finally Gerry announces we're done. Just as we're about to get the lift down to the exit, I realize I'm desperate for the loo.

He uses his card to let me back through the door. 'All the way to the end, then it's just round the corner. I'll wait here with your mother.'

The door clicks shut quietly behind me, the sound of my fate being sealed.

CHAPTER 6

My trainers squeak on the shiny white floor of the corridor. I walk to the end and turn the corner. There's the scent of something chemical, probably from the toilets up ahead. I've found that I can encourage my newfound senses with a little attention to the passage of air over the tiny hairs in my nostrils as I breathe in. It's not blindsiding me so much. Surely that's a good thing. Ingrid would tell me to distract myself, but I don't want to. Where's the harm, when there's nobody around?

Except, I realize, right now, there is someone around.

With a jolt, I understand two things. First, I'm back in Barb's corridor. The door to Room 909 is just a few metres ahead, propped open slightly by a metal container the size of a shoebox. Second, someone is in the room. I can hear them clattering about.

I hesitate in front of the toilet door.

The hairs on my neck rise and I stop, sniff. It's Owen.

Didn't he say he was on his way out? He left when we did. Why's he gone back?

Softly, I walk further down the corridor, closer to Room 909 until I'm just outside. It's definitely him. His sweat reeks of anxiety and adrenaline. My field of vision narrows, focused on his shadow moving across the brightness of the gap.

There's a rucksack on the floor by his feet too, slightly open. A glimpse of red balls packed in plastic. Barb's food?

Then the door opens wider as he leans out to put something in the box. He's wearing long white gloves that go all the way up his arms. And, squirming in his grip, is Barb. He holds her with one hand, and carefully opens the box with the other, struggling slightly in the thick gloves. As he does so, he glances up, and our eyes meet. He goes still.

A long second passes. I can see him wondering whether to say something or let me ask what he's up to. I'm making the same calculation.

And then the decision is taken away from both of us. It seems to happen in slow motion. Barb wrenches out of his grasp. She's twisting in the air, and his gloved hands are clutching desperately at nothing. Then she's coming down, landing on his shoulder and slithering down the outside of his lab coat. Before he can grab her, she disappears inside the glove.

Owen lets out an unearthly yell, ripping at it. 'No, no, no, no, no!'

He finally throws the glove off and it hits the wall, drops to the floor with a heavy slap.

We both stare at his arm.

Barb has wrapped herself around it just above the elbow, pulsating gently, slowly tightening. In a panic, Owen digs at her, trying to get his fingers underneath to peel her off, to no effect. His forehead is shiny with sweat, his breath coming in terrified pants.

'I'll get help,' I yell, turning away to speed round the corner. Gerry and Mum are only seconds away.

But my body jolts to a halt. Owen's hand has shot out and grabbed my arm, his fingers strong around my wrist.

'Get off!'

I throw my weight back towards him, trying to make him lose his balance. It works – he falls flat on the polished floor, but he doesn't let go, and I tumble on top of him, my arm twisting painfully beneath me. I struggle to move away but he still has me, both of us lying sprawled on the floor. His face is inches from mine – his eyes wild and glittering.

'Let go! What are you doing?'

As I watch, Barb loosens her grip slightly on Owen's arm. Her sinuous grey body begins to wind a path up towards his wrist. Towards the hand that is still tightly holding on to my arm.

I pull away with all my strength, yanking my arm practically out of its socket, grunting with effort, but he's way too strong. I'm powerless, able only to watch as Barb slides over Owen's knuckles, moving with those hundreds of tiny openings along her entire body.

My skin crawls with revulsion. I cannot bear the thought of her touching me.

She slows as she approaches my bare forearm.

A hair's breadth from contact, she snaps away from me like an elastic band, so fast and hard that she hits Owen in the face, then drops to the floor. But immediately she's twisting and sliding on the polished surface, propelling herself back towards him.

This time he's faster. Still on the floor, he lunges, grabs her with the hand that still has the glove on. There's a struggle as he fights to contain her, but finally, on all fours, hunched over the metal box with his back towards me, he slams the lid on it and throws the catch.

For a second we both stay there, panting. The scent of his relief washes over me. Then he's staggering up, holding the box, heading for the fire exit.

I can't let him take her. Gerry said she's the only one left. Without her, their best hope for a cure is gone.

Ingrid's face flashes into my mind. *In a heartbeat.*

Before I know what I'm doing, just as he pushes the fire door, I reach out to stop him, grasping at his open lab coat. There's a tearing sound. He whirls round, clutching at his side, crying out in pain, dropping the box. A red stain begins to seep through his fingers. There are four short, deep cuts to one side of his stomach, just above the hip.

For a moment I'm confused.

Then I look down at my arm. Except it's not my arm. At least, not all of it. Up to my wrist, it's the same as ever, but instead of my fingers, there are four Ripper claws. The tips are shiny, wet. Dripping red.

I blink and they're gone, and there's only my chewed nails, though they're sticky with blood.

Those gashes on his belly came from me.

I stagger back. The whole corridor is flashing light and dark as my brain jerks between Ripper and human, like I'm on a spinning bumper car. An alarm goes off somewhere. It grows faint and then unbearably loud from one second to the next and back again.

This can't be happening. The full moon is nearly two weeks away.

There's a crash some distance behind me, a door slamming. I drag my eyes away from my own hands. Owen is backing away, clutching his wound. His blood drips onto the shiny white floor, his shoes sliding on it. Then he blinks, seems to wake up, and reaches for the box again. I leap for it but he gets there before me and I miss, skidding on his blood, falling flat on my face.

From just behind me comes Gerry's voice, calling my name.

'He's got her,' I manage. 'He's got Barb.'

'Owen! What do you think you're playing at?!'

Gerry moves in front of the fire exit, holding his

fists out awkwardly, like he watched *Rocky* once. Owen sneers.

'Playing? Get real. I'm the only one taking her seriously. She's wasted on you. You're a joke, Gerry. Get out of my way. She's coming with me.'

'Don't do this.' Gerry glances down at me. 'Are you hurt, Sel?'

My lips feel weird and bubbly, and the muscles all over my body are snapping and popping like firecrackers. It's like my flesh is glitching. I try to tell him not to worry about me but now my tongue is swollen and useless in my mouth. My jaw aches, my muscles stretch, my chin bones lengthen and the skin on my face tingles as hairs sprout. My head is wolfing out. I see him take it in. His eyes widen in shock.

Owen takes the chance to make his move. He shoves hard into Gerry with his whole body, pushing them both through the fire exit out of sight.

I need to get a grip. Head pounding, I struggle onto all fours, go to wipe my fringe out of my face and nearly poke my own wolfish eye out – the claws are back, for now.

Heavy footsteps pound behind me, and two security guards run past and follow Gerry through the fire exit. The second one does a double take as he catches sight of me, but follows his colleague.

I stagger after them, my focus billowing wider and narrower, colours bleeding in and out. They're running down the stairs ahead of me, which wind in a tight square past the lower three floors. But as I look over the handrail, all the way down the drop to the ground floor, my stomach lurches.

Gerry is lying at the bottom. He must have fallen, or been pushed over. His legs are splayed unnaturally.

I make it down the stairs fast, reaching him the same time as the security guards do. They're already on their radios calling for an ambulance. I run past them to the cool air outside, and look all around, but there's no sign of Owen. An engine growls, and I just catch a glimpse of a car speeding through the gates, and out down the country lane. The security guard at the gatehouse runs out, several seconds too late.

There's chaos for a few minutes – staff running, more alarms sounding, sirens approaching and whizzing off again in pursuit. Slowly, my breathing returns to normal, my vision calms. I'm no longer looking down a long furry muzzle but a blurry pink nose. I clutch at myself in panic, but my clothes are intact, other than my sleeves – the rest of me never Ripped out.

'Sel!' Mum runs towards me from the building. She flings her arms around me, and I wrap mine around her. One of them is fully human, the other not so much, but it's behind her back, and she doesn't spot it. I close my eyes briefly in relief.

When I open them, one of the security guards has his phone out taking a photo.

CHAPTER 7

Thursday 31 January

I persuade Mum to let me have a few days off school, after such a traumatic experience. But I can't avoid it for ever.

I wake up the next day well before dawn after a fretful night of weird dreams in which parts of me Turned and Returned explosively at the most inappropriate moments – in Maths, on the sports field, shopping, on the toilet – and my heart starts hammering in my chest. Everyone will be asking questions about me but no one, least of all me, has any answers. The only person who might, Gerry, is lying unconscious in hospital.

Nothing like this has happened to Ingrid yet, but we both know it must be on the cards. I've begged her to stay quiet about her own symptoms.

You'd think the main news would be the theft of Barb, and the efforts being made to get her back so that research can be continued. Or at least to get her *corpse* back – because the official view is that she won't have survived. There's no public detail on what she is, or exactly what might happen if she *is* still alive, just that she's a 'missing lab specimen' which requires very particular conditions, and that she's crucial in the search for a cure. They're playing down any risk of an outbreak of Frozen Fever. I suppose they don't want to cause panic.

Work on the cure is supposedly still ongoing, but it's clear that without Barb, and without Gerry for the time being, they're pretty much back to square one.

I'm not so sure about Barb being dead. Owen knew more than anyone about her, except maybe Gerry. If anyone can keep her alive, it's him. He certainly seemed to think he could.

Why, though? What's he planning to do with her? It sounded like he was frustrated with Gerry. Maybe he's got his own secret little lab somewhere and plans to pop up with a cure one day, and get all the credit. Or is he just a maniac, planning to use Barb as a biological weapon or something?

But it's not the theft of Barb that's taking up most airtime. No, my little fur-and-claws incident is *much* more dramatic and entertaining. It's all over the internet, in the form of the security guard's photo. My hairy arm across Mum's back, claws extended, me staring over her shoulder at the camera with a slight frown that, I have to admit, does make me look villainous.

At least they haven't linked my mini Rip-out to my having been bitten by the Revenant. Which means they haven't linked it to Ingrid, either. That's the extent of the good news. The rest is bad.

My time as a hero is officially over.

I've had to confess to Mum about my on-off increased senses. I play it down as much as possible, but she's not best pleased I never mentioned it before.

Gerry's team at Probius have asked if I'll come in to be examined, though they need time to figure out the appropriate tests. I felt I had to say yes, though I'm hoping Gerry'll be out of hospital by the time they're ready. He's the only one I was ready to trust.

On a TV breakfast news programme this morning, one of the Probius team that I don't recall meeting is on as a guest. She says it's possible I have a completely different version of the virus, and that I should be examined as soon as possible. She's insistent that my condition can't be infectious, because we'd know by now if it was, but then ruins things by going on to suggest we call it *corpus monstrum*. I really hope that doesn't catch on.

Before the day's out I've been questioned by the police – not Sergeant Trash, but proper ones who come out from Norstead, the town closest to Probius. I'm not a suspect, only a witness, but you wouldn't think it from the way some people are looking at me.

Not surprisingly, Sherman's absolutely furious. He's been loudly demanding that the regional authorities put every resource into chasing down Owen and retrieving

Barb. To be fair, I think they're doing their best with the stretched resources they have. They've promised to send out drones, organize special ops in a couple of places where Owen has links. But Owen has disappeared. There are rumours he's fled into the lawless countryside up north but no one has produced evidence of that.

Sherman hasn't specifically accused me of anything, but he doesn't need to. The speculation about me on his channel, Facts Unleashed, has made it one of the most viewed on the internet. The forums are practically on fire. Mum asked him to moderate them to take down some of the horrible stuff about me, but he refused, citing freedom of speech.

When you write the facts down, it's easy to make them look bad:

I'm famously at least in part responsible for the Rippocalypse.

I've been defending Turning and have made no secret I'm not interested in a cure.

Apparently, I can semi-Turn outside of a full moon, unlike anyone else.

Owen stole Barb when I just happened to be in the lab.

Gerry – the person who knows most about *corpus pilori* and was working for the cure – is badly injured, in hospital. No one saw exactly how he ended up at the bottom of the stairs.

SEL ARCHER LAB RAID – COINCIDENCE?
YOU DECIDE

That's the title of one of the many, many threads on Facts Unleashed.

Lack of any actual evidence or proof is no barrier to belief, apparently. According to them, the fact they can't prove anything against me just goes to show how careful I've been in covering my tracks.

The accusations and ridiculous theories pile up. I secretly hired Owen. I've been working away in a hidden lab of my own to upgrade myself, because I want to be a Ripper all the time.

I try cutting through the avalanche of hostility, posting comments in my own defence from my anonymous account, pretending to be a neutral observer. It only results in scorn:

> How thick r u? Wake up sheeple

> Being a 15yo boy is the PERFECT cover. No
> one wd suspect!

At least it's only me that's the object of these attacks. It's pretty lonely, but I couldn't handle the guilt of dragging any of my friends into it.

At the weekend, Mum hits me with the news that she's going to visit Mika's family in the new town, Greenvale, for a few days. Lucas is going, too, leaving Pedro and Elena.

'You're kidding me. Now? With all this going on? You're

just going to abandon me so you can check out Mika's new house?'

This is not like her. I was expecting her to be watching my every move like an overanxious hawk.

She sighs through her nose, exasperated. 'I'm not abandoning you. It's only a few days. You're perfectly capable. There's plenty of food in the fridge. Just make sure you get yourself to school on time.'

'Why's Lucas going?'

'He'd like to see them, too.' She shrugs, like it's no big deal. But she won't look me in the eye as she says it. Something's definitely going on with those two. In fact, nothing has ever been more obvious. I don't even mind, to be honest – he's a good guy, and I already feel like I'm related to Elena and Pedro anyway. But I'm pretty hurt that she thinks right now is a good time for a romantic weekend, just when my life is imploding.

I go back to school on Monday, and get a whole load of curiosity, plus a few suspicious looks. To my relief, the people I consider any kind of friends mostly think my semi-Rip-out was kind of cool, and they want to know how I did it.

Elena tells me Sherman is keeping an especially tight rein on Ben now, warning him that I'm a bad influence. I can't even text him, because his dad has taken to checking his phone. Apparently Sherman asked him if I'd revealed any clue that I was planning a heist on the lab. Elena says Ben is trying to argue it's nonsense, but I already know that battle is lost. Sherman won't listen. I need to grab a chance to talk to Ben in person, at school, but it's not easy when we're not in the same year, and since Sherman's the caretaker, he's always stalking the corridors.

In the midst of all this, I get another postcard from Slay PR, Jim and Tom sympathizing and saying they'll always be there for me. Not right now, guys.

The only worrying new thing is that I notice that the Alliance have started carrying their guns around openly. They used to at least be a little bit discreet about it, but some of them are strolling around like they're in a first-person shooter game. Mayor Warren apparently had a meeting with them to tell them it was unacceptable, but came out like a kicked puppy, tail between his legs. I don't know what power they've got over him but he's agreed to leave them be, says it's temporary and they only have our best interests at heart. What with Probius being attacked, the Alliance feel the situation has escalated. They think they need to step things up to keep disorder out of Tremorglade.

There's no disorder, though. They're the ones making everyone feel uncomfortable.

So Monday passes unremarkably. Tuesday is much the same. Wednesday there's a big Alliance protest outside Mayor Warren's office, but it fizzles out into nothing.

It's not till Thursday that things take a turn for the worse.

CHAPTER 8

Thursday 7 February

I spend a long time in the shower, seeing if I can make myself Turn again. The more I think about it, the more I realize suppressing it is a bad idea. It's *control* that I need. If I know how to start it, I have a much better chance of finding out how to stop it.

It's a good thing nobody can see me grimacing and striking aggressive poses. I even try grabbing my own throat. It's not a great success. There's a tingling on my skin that might be a little frisson of fur trying to come up, or might just be the mint shower gel. The most I can do is summon my Ripper hearing for a short time, and it comes with Ripper eyesight, which is okay if you want to see fast-moving small objects at night, less so if you're trying to shave for the first time.

Eventually I give up trying to make my claws spring

out, and just try to relax under the warm water. I've been so eaten up with anxiety lately, it feels like my human body is held together by stress.

This is what Ingrid doesn't understand.

Before she got bitten, she was already an athlete. I bet she never fell over putting her trousers on in a hurry. She didn't knock all the hurdles down on sports day, could be trusted not to break fragile objects just by looking at them.

All my life I've been the clumsy one, the guy who accidentally shot his teacher with a tranq dart, the kid who doesn't notice he's walking round with a ketchup stain down his T-shirt, the boy who always gets picked last in PE. Yes, I know I sound whiny, and no, it was never a big deal. Until now. Because now, on Howl nights, for the first time in my life, my body does what I tell it to do, in the way I tell it to, and I can't get enough of it.

As a Ripper, I'm strong, capable, fast. Yes, I've made mistakes, maybe gone too far on occasion. But at last, Sel Archer might actually have a worthwhile skill. I just wish I'd been able to use it effectively at the lab, in time to protect Gerry, and Barb. If only I had let myself explore my abilities earlier, practise them, maybe I could have stopped it happening.

Out in the world, there are murderers and robbers, there are conspiracy theorists whipping up hatred, there's Sherman trying to persuade everybody that fur is fatal. But instead of worrying about them, everybody's obsessed with me.

The whole situation is screwed up.

I'm not the dangerous one.

» » »

It's not easy to locate Ben at school. But I finally spot him in the corridor at lunchtime and we manage to slip into the DT classroom. I glance around outside before closing the door and pulling the blind down. The place stinks of sawdust and hot metal from the previous lesson. The first years have been learning to use the saws.

We fist-bump sadly, then he shakes his head and goes for a hug. 'I've missed you. Dad is totally out of control right now. His blood pressure is through the roof. You wouldn't believe—'

I throw off his arms in horror and step back, stumbling, off balance. He's still talking but I'm not listening. 'Woah, woah.'

He laughs, confused. 'It's just a hug, bro!'

I shake my head, half choking, too shocked to speak.

'You okay? Did something go down the wrong way? Do you need me to do the Heimlich thing?'

I shake my head again. I still can't talk for a second. This doesn't make any sense.

He glances down at my feet. 'Did I step on your toe?'

'No, no.'

'Then what—'

'Shh.' Warily, I draw closer to him again. He shrinks back as I sniff his neck.

'What are you—'

'Shh. It was there, but I've lost it. Stay still.'

I expand my nostrils and take a slow breath in, under his ear. There it is again. Just a trace.

'You're being really weird, you know,' he says, but he doesn't move, his eyes sliding round to watch me, worried now.

The pores in his skin begin to fill, tiny amounts of sweat oozing to the surface, and all at once I get it full in the face: salt, ammonia, little micronutrients, metabolic waste and ... oh no. 'What the—'

'Okay you're scaring me.'

'Your sweat. It's ... no way.'

'Hey, I had a shower this morning, it can't be that bad.' He sniffs his armpit warily. 'Is it?'

'No, I mean ... it's ...' I'm struggling to get the words out. 'You're not Immutable anymore.'

He blinks at me. 'That's impossible.'

'I'm certain.' I've never been surer of anything. People who Turn smell of *corpus pilori* – more so when they're Rippers, but even as humans. I can always tell who's Immutable and who isn't. Ben was.

Now, he isn't.

But it's worse than that.

Ingrid and I smell different from the others. *Extra* has a unique kick to it. When I breathe Ingrid in, there's a distinct, half-sweet, half-bitter aroma, and I have the same scent. It's unmistakable.

And it's what Ben smells like right now.

It makes no sense.

Wait …

'Give me your hand.' I grab his left, scan it. Nothing. Then his right … and there it is. My thumb traces the brown skin on the back of his wrist, where there's a barely visible line of darker spots, almost-healed marks.

It's where my teeth must have sunk into his flesh as I pulled him out of the river to safety.

I force my voice to stay level, calm.

'Do you feel odd at all, Ben? Any *extra*-style senses?'

'Don't think so. No. I feel okay.'

Is it possible I'm overreacting? Maybe it's my own *extra pilori* I'm smelling.

But I need to be sure. Something comes back to me. 'You said a minute ago that your dad's blood pressure is through the roof. How do you know?'

He blinks in confusion. 'He's stressed, I guess.'

'Not *why*. I said *how* do you know?'

He frowns. 'Well, I … this morning when we were having breakfast, his pulse sounded …' he trails off, swallows. 'I could just tell,' he finishes, voice suddenly a whisper.

My heart is pounding. What have I done?

70

'That's not normal, is it?' he asks quietly.

I swear under my breath. 'No. Oh, Ben. I'm sorry.'

His eyes search my face, anxious. 'You think I'm ... like you now?'

I take another long sniff, hoping against hope that I'm wrong. But he reeks of it.

'I'm so, so sorry,' I say again, uselessly. 'I think my teeth just nicked you when I brought you out of the river.' What a way to confirm that *extra* is contagious. It must be in my saliva or something. I never intended to bite him, had no idea I'd done it.

For a long moment, he sits there in silence, staring past me into the corner of the classroom, unfocused. I can almost see the thoughts racing through his mind. I wouldn't blame him if he was angry. Really angry.

But when he finally brings his gaze back to me, there's only fear, not anger.

'Dad is going to lose his mind.'

'He won't find out. It'll be okay. Keep calm. You can hide it.'

'Like you did?' A nervous mini-laugh escapes Ben.

It's a fair point.

'The lab was a very specific situation. Ingrid hasn't had anything like that happen yet. I think it's because I was in danger. And I can learn to control it. It's not that bad.'

Ben's not listening. He stands up shakily, hands running over his head, turning away. 'Not that bad? Never mind super-senses or whatever this is. Sel, if you're right, next Howl night my dad is going to see me transform into a Ripper – the thing he hates most in the world.'

I bring him around to face me, put my hands firmly on his shoulders, force him to look at me. 'Listen. It's going to be okay. We'll help you. Your dad never has to find out you're any kind of a Ripper now. Let alone—'

Ben says, 'Dad.'

I freeze. He's staring over my shoulder towards the doorway.

I don't want to look, but all the same, I twist to follow his gaze to where Sherman is standing, completely still. All the blood drains from my head. How long has he been there? What did he hear?

He doesn't leave me wondering for long.

With a roar, he picks up a chair, throws it in one movement. Shock makes me slow to move, and it hits me a glancing blow on my temple before clattering to the floor. Ben screams, 'Dad, no!'

Sherman's coming at me, his face purple with rage, fists clenched.

I slide behind a table and dodge one way, then the other, as he comes after me.

'WHAT HAVE YOU DONE?' He's yelling, his voice cracked, his face contorted with fury and anguish. Ben is shouting, pulling at his dad desperately but to no effect.

Sherman bellows, 'My son! My son! My son!' over and

over like it's one endless word, stripped of all meaning by incoherent rage. Tears are streaming down his cheeks.

Somewhere in the corridor, voices are approaching, feet running closer.

Ben is dragging at his dad's clothes, trying to stop him coming after me, but I'm backed into a corner now.

Sherman's eyes are bulging, his mouth twisted into a gritted snarl.

I hold my own hands out in front of me to shield myself, and as I do so, static crackles all down my arm, the hairs springing to attention.

Uh-oh.

It can't happen now. It mustn't. Once is a mistake, twice looks deliberate. I brace myself to resist it, and I'm succeeding. Energy is pulsing through me but I'm holding on to it, refusing to let it off its leash as it bucks and kicks, demanding to be free.

Sherman grabs my wrist and squeezes so I cry out in pain.

'You're coming with me, boy. You need to be caged before you can do any more damage.'

'Calm down, Dad, calm down.' Ben's voice is hoarse, yelling in panic.

Sherman's fingernails dig into my skin as he pulls me away from the wall, dragging me across the classroom, tripping as I go. My tingling muscles strain to answer him back, shriek to assert themselves. I bang my knee, hard, on the corner of a table and the pain shoots through me like lightning.

Between one heartbeat and the next, I lose it.

Out of the corner of my eye, I see the arm of my shirt balloon, then shred from shoulder to cuff. Ripper fur erupts from my elbow up through my wrist, my hand swelling into a great paw, claws springing out like flick-knives. Sherman cries out as they slice into his fingers, his skin unzipping, blood welling up. He drops his hands. But his movements are slow, compared to mine. I'm already reaching for his neck before I know what I'm doing, my arm muscles contracting ready for the decisive swipe.

Then Ben is there, in between us, his arm protectively across his dad, screaming. I manage to pull back at the last millisecond, one claw just catching at my friend's shirtsleeve before I wrench myself backwards.

For a moment we stand there breathing hard, Ben's sleeve hanging in two parts, showing just how close I came to cutting his dad's throat.

My arm Rip-out is already diminishing, the hairs sinking back into my skin, power ebbing away. I blink and my fingernails are back.

I'm shaking with adrenaline.

I glance at the doorway. It's crowded with students who came to see what all the noise was but are too scared to come in, and a teacher or two trying to get a glimpse over their heads. There are a couple of phones out, recording.

74

I hope at least they got it from the start. Sherman will be in big trouble now. Even in my school, grown men throwing chairs and dragging students around is not acceptable. He'll be fired, for sure.

But that doesn't change the awful thing: that I've given Ben *extra pilori*.

Another thought looms, though. A selfish, scared one.

This is not going to look good, for me.

I thought it couldn't get any worse.

Now, I've brought an Immutable over to the hairy side. And not just any Immutable, but the son of the founder of the Alliance.

I didn't bite Sherman, but I almost wish I had. Getting infected himself might have changed his perspective. As things stand, I'm toast.

We both are.

CHAPTER 9

Friday 8 February

'I can't leave you alone for five minutes, can I?' Mum said, calling me just as I got home. School had already rung her to let her know the situation. I resisted telling her that I did warn her not to leave me.

This morning, I'm woken by the doorbell. I'm about to trudge grumpily down to open it, assuming it's a parcel, but change my mind after a glance from my bedroom window: there are reporters outside my house. I creep down and lock the door.

Apparently, they've got hold of Mum's phone number, too, as she tells me when she rings again, even more upset. They've left her voice messages, asking things like, 'Is your son dangerous, Mrs Archer? Do you have any comment on this claim that Sel has found a way to infect Immutables?'

Sherman has no such hesitation about talking to the reporters. He's been fired, at least. But when I switch on the TV, there he is being interviewed, saying I must have attacked Ben, to infect him on purpose. Everything is twisted. Instead of my bear defence and river rescue being heroic, now they're evidence I'm a bloodthirsty monster.

They grill an expert from Probius – the same woman on Gerry's team who insisted I couldn't be infectious. To be fair to her, she doesn't roll over. She doubles down on what she said: 'There's no reason to panic – there is no *evidence* that any other person has actually been infected with this mutation. We only have an allegation. Definitive test results will take a while. We won't know for sure until Howl night, when the alleged newly infected person's status will become clear.' She's certain they'll figure out what's up with me, but it's going to take a while. To my enormous relief, she rejects out of hand Sherman's suggestion that they should forcibly isolate me somewhere in the lab. They don't believe it's necessary to lock me up.

I'm grateful. As the one organization that is trying to find a cure, Probius's words hold weight. Sherman may not agree, but I suspect their public support of me is all that's standing in the way of his coming over here with a tranq dart and a cage.

I'm temporarily suspended from school, mainly because of pressure from other parents. Partially Ripping out at the lab was one thing. But potentially passing on a new, unknown brand of *pilori* to my classmates, their own kids? That's a whole different matter.

I've had loads of messages from friends, saying they're really sorry but they're not allowed to go near me for now. It's nothing personal.

Towards the evening, most of the reporters give up and head home, but there are still a couple of die-hard stragglers, hunched up against the cold, sipping from steaming mugs. Ingrid, Pedro and Elena all offer to come over, but I say no, not while those guys are still there. I don't want my friends shouted at or harassed. No one has heard from Ben since yesterday. His phone is turned off, and all our messages have gone unread.

Ingrid bravely knocked on his front door, and Sherman came out and told her to stay away. He said the only way he'll ever want to see us is if we turn up holding a cure. Just before he slammed the door, he said that Ben hates me and never wants to see me again, or anyone who calls themselves my friend.

I don't believe that. Ingrid saw Ben watching from his bedroom window at the front of the house as she was leaving. He put his hand up to the glass, but then quickly disappeared, maybe hearing his dad come upstairs. I can't imagine what's going on in there, but I feel awful. On Howl night, Ben will be alone in a cage.

» » »

I heat up a curry in the microwave and eat it sitting at the kitchen table, feeling sorry for myself. It's so quiet. I'm lonely. Mum insisted on taking Eddie with her on her visit to Greenvale, since it wouldn't be fair to leave him alone all day while I was at school.

Before bed, she calls again and we have a long conversation. She's no calmer than this morning. She's angry with school, for suspending me, and she's none too impressed with Mayor Warren, whom she calls weak. I let her rant, expecting her to get around to telling me she's on her way home, but then she says, 'Sel, I've found somewhere to live, here in Greenvale. So has Lucas. Not together, I mean. Separately.' I can hear her embarrassment over the phone. But I couldn't care less about how cosy she and Lucas are.

'You ... you're leaving me here?'

She laughs. 'Oh, Sel, don't be ridiculous. Of course not. I've been worried for a while now about the direction Tremorglade is headed. I hear things. Sherman has influence. The Alliance are saying they've no confidence in Mayor Warren's ability to keep them safe. They want something done about you. I'm worried he's going to take matters into his own hands. It's become too dangerous.'

I knew it. I knew she wasn't merely on a jolly visit to Mika's parents.

'So we're just going to run away?' I can't believe what I'm hearing.

'It's not safe for you in Tremorglade.'

'But ... Mika says Greenvale is only half built. It's practically empty. And what about Ingrid?'

'I've already spoken to Bernice and Amy. They're planning to move out too, with all the Juniper kids, but it'll take a while longer to make arrangements for them.'

I'm too shocked to speak. I knew Bernice and Amy were concerned but I had no idea this was on the cards. It seems like the adults have been discussing this for a while. Maybe even before what happened at the lab.

Everything's moving so fast, my mind can't process it.

'Lucas has spoken with Pedro. Pedro's going to drive you and Elena out to Hastaville tomorrow, and I'll come and pick you up from there a day or so later.'

'Tomorrow!'

'Sel, I'm not taking no for an answer on this.'

'Then Ingrid needs to come with us.'

She sighs. 'That's up to her guardians. But fine with me. Pedro can take you all in his car. Don't hang about.'

'What about Ben? We can't just leave him here.'

'I'm sorry, Sel, but there's nothing we can do to help him. He's Sherman's son.'

'But ...'

'While you're there, the Alliance have a villain to blame. Maybe leaving will help calm things down. I'm not saying it has to be for ever. But the kindest thing we can do for him is leave.'

She finishes by telling me to go stay over the road at the Torres house tonight, with Elena and Pedro. Maybe she's being overcautious, but she says our house might be a target.

After she rings off, I sit there with my head in my hands.

The worst of it is, she's right. Me being here is making Ben's life worse. If I leave, maybe Sherman will at least let him outside again.

But there's no way I'm leaving Ingrid behind. I'm certain I can persuade Bernice and Amy to let her come with us.

I message Ingrid. She replies that we should talk about it in person, but insists, in ALL CAPS, that I shouldn't leave the house. She'll come to me in the morning. Fine.

I'm about to start packing when the doorbell rings, making me jump.

Peeking through the living-room curtains, I don't see anyone standing outside. The dark street looks completely empty. All the same, I wait a few minutes before going to open the door, just a crack.

There's no one there. Silence.

I'm about to close the door again when a shape on the porch step catches my eye. There's something small, furry and covered in blood. A dead squirrel. A tent peg is stuck through it, with a printed note.

I bend down and, with shaking hands, pull the note off without touching the dead creature.

SEL ARCHER
BETRAYER OF HUMANITY
DEATH IS COMING

CHAPTER 10

Ingrid

Saturday 9 February

You think you know a place, when you've grown up there. But its character can change, more quickly than you believe possible. Suddenly the home you thought you knew inside out feels very different.

School won't be opening on Monday, until further notice. Apparently, a group of parents complained that their children didn't feel safe there anymore. Sel wasn't mentioned by name, but it was obvious who they meant. Rumour is that they're accusing the head of knowing all about 'a student's infectious condition' but still allowing him to attend. And then anonymous threats against staff started arriving. It doesn't take a genius to work out who's behind it all.

There's a bitter smell on the air when I leave for the Torres house. A charcoal stench that persists even in the drizzle falling from the grey sky. It catches in the back of my throat, claggy and thick, and only gets stronger as I walk.

Approaching Jenny's bakery, I slow. Sel's mum has owned it just since the Rippocalypse, but she's been building up a nice business, turning a profit. It's a warm, welcoming, neat place that normally has tempting pastries on display. Now, splattered across the shuttered windows, bright red graffiti reads *MOTHER OF THE BEAST*. It's a punch to my gut. This must have happened last night. I'm so glad she's not here to see it, having shut up shop for a few days while she went to Greenvale.

An elderly couple are standing there, tutting at the mess. I stop and stare, too. The woman is saying how awful it is, how there's no need for violence, then she adds, ' ... but you can understand why people are upset. That boy shouldn't just be allowed to run amok ...'

I don't wait to hear any more.

Turning the corner to pass by the mayor's office in the square, I finally see the source of the smell – two burnt-out cars, blackened and destroyed.

I knew there had been some kind of noisy disturbance here last night, with a group of Immutable Alliance protesting, unhappy with what they call Mayor Warren's failure to take action against unspecified 'threats' in Tremorglade. It's kind of impressive how a group wandering around with guns can claim they're the vulnerable ones.

A couple of Alliance men are chatting, balaclavas off, standing next to one of the cars. I put my hood up and walk faster, hoping to avoid their attention.

It doesn't work.

'Miss?' one calls. I hear his boots clumping across the square towards me. I turn, shoulders tense, but he's smiling, proffering a choice of stickers in his black-gloved hand. *Proudly Human! Immutable Alliance 4Eva! Make Humanity Hairless Again! Fur is Fatal!*

'Hey, have one of these. For free.' He winks, like he's doing me a favour.

'No, thanks.' I try to walk on, but he shifts in front of me.

'I'd recommend it. Stick one on your car.'

'I'm not old enough to drive.'

He laughs. 'Well, your bike, then. Or even your cute little self. Here. I'm Dan, by the way. And you are?' He peels off the backing from one and goes to put it on my coat. I jerk back.

'I said no.'

Off to my left, the other guy saunters closer, hands in his pockets. He moves behind me, just out of my line of view.

Dan regards me for a moment, his smile dropping slightly. 'Just take one. Protects you from people getting the wrong idea, if you know what I mean.' His eyes flick to the blackened cars. I'm guessing they didn't have stickers on.

I swallow.

'Unless...' he trails off, eyes narrowing. 'Do I know you?'

'No.' I go to walk past him again but this time he puts out an arm to stop me. The other guy is close behind me now, and my senses flicker into life. I can hear his breath, smell him. I don't like the odour developing from both of them. Anticipation. Growing excitement.

Before I can react, my hood is flipped down from behind. I grab at air, too late.

'You look familiar,' Dan says. He's a newbie to town, but maybe he'll have seen my picture at some point, as one of the original Tremorglade Four.

I shake my head. 'We've never met. I'm supposed to be visiting a friend. Just let me go.'

He tips his head on one side. 'Would that be Sel, now?'

Damn. He's recognized me.

'You can't keep me here,' I say, trying to keep the tremble out of my voice. 'You're not in charge.'

'That's where you're wrong,' says the voice behind me. I resist the urge to turn. 'Haven't you heard? The mayor left town last night. Ran away. Sherman's in charge. He'll take the security of this town seriously.'

My heart starts thudding against my ribcage.

'There are laws. You can't just take over—'

'Yeah? Who says so?' Dan looks around quizzically. 'I don't see anyone coming to stop us, do you, Bri?'

Bri sniggers.

'Thing is, no one else wants to get involved in a place like Tremorglade, anymore. Mutant monsters, kids spreading disease ... The police in Hastaville literally put out a statement saying they don't cover this area.'

'We have our own police,' I insist.

'Who, Sergeant Hale? Oh, yeah, he works for us now.'

I stare at him. I know Hale isn't the bravest of people, but I'm so disappointed in him.

'Listen, if you and your friends don't like it, you're free to leave,' he sneers.

'Maybe we should just bring them in,' says Bri behind me. 'All of them. I know Sherman said not to do anything yet, but here's a bird in the hand ...' He reaches out for my arm.

I don't wait to hear the rest. I whip round and shove him, sending him stumbling backwards, and make a run for it, my trainers slapping on the wet cobbles. I half expect to get a bullet in the back, but instead there's laughter.

'Where are you going?' calls Dan, teasingly.

I run as fast as I can, rain driving into my face now. My hair whips across my eyes and I don't see the wonky paving stone, just feel the sudden jolt to the bones in my foot and then the hard ground wooshing the breath from my lungs. I break my fall with my hands, and brace for a kicking. But it seems they've had their fun. When I look back, they haven't moved.

Slowly, I get to my feet, and hobble away.

Dan calls after me, 'A friendly warning. From tomorrow, the gloves are off.'

» » »

Pedro looks pale and tired when he warily opens the front door to me. 'Hey.'

I wasn't going to tell him what happened on the way here, but my face and my grazed palms must give it away.

'Oh, Ingrid.' He takes me to the kitchen sink and gently runs the tap so I can clean the blood from my hands. 'What happened?'

I fill him in. Warren gone, Hale being on Sherman's payroll. He listens to me, biting a nail, frowning.

'Okay. We're going to wait till it's dark before we go. Better if the Alliance are mostly in bed. I don't fancy running into them on our way out.'

I make a noncommittal noise.

'I'm glad you made it,' he says, when I don't add anything else. 'Elena is packing but his highness is upstairs in my room. Playing games on his laptop, probably. Go on up.'

Sel is indeed on his laptop, lying on Pedro's bed.

He looks up with relief when I enter the room. 'I didn't hear you come in.'

I flump down next to him and look at his screen. 'Why are you on Sherman's site? It's not good for you to read that stuff.' I don't tell him I check it myself, quite often. The usual weirdos have posted on the forum.

> He wants to make everyone the same as him, now. You know how he's always going on about how great Turning is, in his videos. He decided to force it on all of us, all the time. You wait. There'll be more victims. Who knows who else he's bitten?

'Oh, for goodness' sake,' I say quietly.

Sel scrolls down. 'Can you believe these absolute melts?' The thread is degenerating. People get angrier the further it goes down.

> Why hasn't he been arrested?

> Lock him up!!!

> Put him down.

'Look, what about this one?' I say, scrolling to a post that says:

> Sel is innocent. You don't know anything about it. He wouldn't hurt anybody.

He sighs. 'I know that's you, Ingrid. You have the same username on Tremorgossip.'

Busted.

'Let's just turn it off.' I bite my lip. 'We help each other, right? And I know you're trying to protect me, too. You're a good friend.'

'Don't worry about it,' he says, his ears going pink. 'Of course we're friends.' He looks intently at the screen, swallows hard. 'But, you know I really—'

I jump up as, faintly, a couple of streets away, there's the sound of glass breaking, an alarm, a *woosh* and the sound of running feet and laughter. Another vehicle set on fire. I shiver. What if they do that to Pedro's car? How will they get out?

Sel catches my eye and smiles wryly. 'Pedro went out and put an Alliance sticker on his, just in case.' He looks at me more closely. 'You okay? Something happen?'

I shrug the question off, not wanting to go into it again. I'm exhausted, on edge, looking out for any signs I might start to Rip out, squashing them the moment they appear. It seems to be working. Sometimes I wonder if, eventually, I could stop myself Ripping out even on Howl nights, just through willpower. That feels more possible than telling Sel what I need to tell him right now.

'Play *Karmic Invasion* with me,' Sel says suddenly. 'You brought your laptop, right?'

'Uh …'

He frowns. 'Didn't you bring your bag?'

I hesitate, trying to find the words. But as I watch, he realizes on his own.

I'm not coming to Greenvale.

» » »

Sel's staring at me hopelessly, out of steam, half an hour of arguing having done nothing to budge me from my decision. We're both standing, facing each other like a couple of boxers catching their breath.

'Bernice and Amy will let you go.'

'Yes. But I'm staying.'

'It makes no sense! You're in danger, too.'

'Sherman hasn't threatened me, specifically. It's you who bit his son.'

'Look around! It's going to get worse. There's nothing here for you.'

'I know. But I'll go with Bernice and Amy and the others from Juniper.'

'Why won't you come now?'

'Because of Ben. I want to make sure he's okay.'

He flinches. 'You think I don't? But we can't get to him.'

'*You* can't. I think I can, especially if you're not here.'

'How?'

'Don't worry about it. Leave it to me.'

He growls in frustration. 'So now you're keeping secrets from me. You said we'd get through this together.'

'We will, but that's *all* of us together. Including Ben.'

'Then I'll stay too.' His jaw sets stubbornly. 'Not everyone in town is on Sherman's side. I'll work harder to get people's support.'

'Oh, please. What are you going to do, hire Slay PR? An ad campaign showing you cuddling kittens is not going to cut it, Sel.'

'No, but—'

'I need you to leave.' My voice comes out harsher than I intended, and he blinks, like I've slapped him. 'Can't you trust me?'

His shoulders sag, defeated.

'When will you come?'

'Bernice says in a few days.'

'Why won't you tell me your plan?'

I hesitate. 'Because you won't like it.'

'Oh, even better.'

He turns and walks a few steps away from me, agitated. 'What if Sherman comes for you, when I'm gone? You won't defend yourself.'

'Excuse me?' I scoff. 'Taekwondo champion, here. You better believe I'll defend myself.'

'But not as much as you could,' he insists. 'We're capable of so much more, now. I don't understand why you refuse to even practise. You have claws, he doesn't. And surely pushing it all back down just makes it more dangerous. I'm sure suppressing must be bad for you.'

A hot flush of anger in my chest. 'So is that why I keep half-Ripping out? Oh, hang on, that's you.'

He has the grace to look embarrassed, but insists, 'I'm getting better at it. Honestly, I really think it's possible to turn it on and off. Just do it when you're on your own, locked in your room. Where's the harm in that?'

I clamp my jaw and glare at him.

He sighs, and his gaze lingers on my eyes, moves over my cheeks, my lips, like he's committing it all to memory.

'Ing, please, I'm so worried.' His voice cracks and I melt, a little.

'Worry about yourself, loser.'

Then, unbelievably, he's coming in closer, hand reaching for my chin.

It's not like I'm immune to his charms, doofus that he is. The big brown eyes, the lopsided smile, the fact he can't hide his feelings even when he thinks he is. I feel like I'm standing on a cliff edge, my centre of gravity tipping ... It would be so easy to let him persuade me, to give in, to tell myself it's not so dangerous to experiment with our strange new impulses and powers. Would it be so bad?

An image of Arty swims up into my head. Blood on my claws, in my mouth. That's what can happen. My stomach swoops, the soles of my feet tingling, and I flinch away.

Sel looks so bewildered and lost that I try to make up for it by bringing him in for a back-slapping bro hug. Then I push him firmly away from me again.

'Bye,' I tell him. 'Don't do anything I wouldn't.'

I say it like it's a joke, and not something that keeps me awake at night.

I walk back home the long way round, head bowed into my coat against the cold, and try to push down the flare of anxiety in my gut.

I'm scared for me, and for Ben, for what might happen to us here in this place where lies are taking over.

But I'm more scared for Sel. For what he's capable of.

CHAPTER 11

Sel

There's no one about. Our street is dead, the lights feeble and yellow under a dense, overcast black sky.

Dumping my rucksack viciously in the boot of Pedro's car, I hear a faint crunch from inside it. Probably broke something. I don't care.

I'm scurrying away in the night like I've done something wrong. This place sucks. And I really messed up with Ingrid. My face flushes hot every time I think of it.

I startle as another rucksack thumps down next to mine in the boot. Elena peers thoughtfully at it.

'Well, that's me. You done?'

'Nope.'

She frowns. 'Do you need to go get something?'

I stare angrily into the boot. 'Yeah. Ingrid. Ben.'

'Oh.' She sighs. 'Don't worry. It'll be okay.'

'How is any of this okay?' I snap back.

She raises her palms defensively. 'No need to bite my head off.'

From the front seat, Pedro breaks through the awkward silence. 'Guys. Get in the car.'

I slam the boot closed and look Elena in the eye. 'I know Ingrid's told you to keep an eye on me. Just so we're clear, I don't need a babysitter.'

Elena doesn't deny it. 'She's just worried about you. You've been a bit ... unpredictable lately.'

'Since when was being predictable a good thing?'

That earns me an eye roll. 'Ugh, Sel, you are so—'

'*Get in the car.*'

Something about Pedro's voice tells me he's not just sick of our arguing.

I look round, but at first see nothing. A cat is sitting under the nearest lamppost, washing its paw. Probably congratulating itself on Eddie's departure.

Elena's intake of breath makes me follow her gaze, further up the street. There's a car parked there, in darkness. A monster of a car with bars across the bumper. Was it there before? I don't think so.

As I watch, its lights turn on. An engine revs.

Elena and I both slide into the back seat of Pedro's car without another word.

Pedro meets my eye in the rear-view mirror.

'Belt up.'

We obey as he starts the car and pulls away from the kerb, the slow, smooth motion belying the tension on his face.

As we pass by the other car I get a view of the driver's eyes through the holes in the balaclava, grim and unblinking. Another man in the passenger seat, and at least one more in the back. Sherman's goons. They watch us go, heads turning slowly as Pedro keeps to the 20 mph speed limit, but they don't seem in a hurry to move.

Elena and I turn to watch through the rear windscreen as we pull away towards the crossroads. The car stays where it is.

'Well, that was creepy,' Elena says, but she speaks too soon.

Just as we reach the crossroads ready for the right turn, there's the sound of its engine gunning behind us, tyres skidding on the icy road surface. They're coming.

My throat seizes up with fear but Pedro doesn't need telling. Our wheels spin as he puts his foot down, the little car struggling for purchase before finding its grip and accelerating away.

'What do they want?' Elena's brow is furrowed with anxiety.

'Probably not just to say bye,' Pedro says, glancing in the rear-view mirror every few seconds.

'Watch the road!' Elena yelps as we bounce off the kerb. 'Keep going.'

'Ya think? Don't worry, no stopping for picnics.' He

clamps his lips tight as he yanks the wheel to take the next turn, heading towards the main road that leads out of town, through the forest.

I twist in my seat, hardly daring to look, but unable to take my eyes off the empty stretch of road behind us.

A glow grows opposite the turning and then the two headlights appear, swivelling round to follow us.

'Pedro,' Elena snaps.

He bites his lip. 'I see them.'

One more turn and we're finally on the straight-as-a-die road that runs through the forest. It once ended in rubble and weeds a short distance into the trees, because no one ever ventured down it, but since the Rippocalypse it's been resurfaced. It's wide enough for two lanes, one going in each direction, and is smooth tarmac all the way. Pedro floors it.

Behind us, almost leisurely, the headlights turn to follow.

There's no alternative route, but we all know we have a problem here.

Their car is faster. Pedro's is an old second-hand motor that he bought for occasional trips out of town, and for ferrying elderly neighbours to the shops. The guys behind us in the big car are gaining fast.

Our engine whines as the speedometer ticks around, slowly, then starts to judder. The other car's lights grow large through the back window.

'Drive faster!' Elena screams.

'This is as fast as it goes!' Pedro yells back.

The other car is so close now I can hear the occupants laughing, through the open window. The big car starts to shift over to the right to come alongside, but Pedro moves over too, almost losing control as he turns the wheel, and only just managing to straighten up. More laughter from behind. Their tyres will have a far better grip on this road.

'We're gonna die,' I moan.

A loud crunch, and we all jerk forward at the nudge from behind. Then a sensation of being pushed along faster than our engine can take us. Pedro lets off a stream of curses, his knuckles pale with gripping the wheel so hard.

We're all out of options. There are no side roads for us to slip onto, no chance to veer off through the forest without crashing straight into a tree. I try to think of all the car chases I've seen in movies, of all the clever escapes, but there's nothing that would work here. We're drifting off the road.

'Brake!' Elena yells, and Pedro's already doing it, trying to slow down and steer straight. If he skidded now we'd spin off the road and be smashed to smithereens against the tree trunks.

Suddenly, blue lights race across our windscreen, chasing each other like fireflies. There's a single *whoop* of a siren – a police car coming up behind us both.

The pressure against our bumper eases. There's a

painful squeal of metal as something rips off either their vehicle or ours. I'm guessing ours.

'It's Hale!' Elena's astonishment speaks for all of us. 'They're stopping. I can't believe it! Let's go! Drive!'

But Pedro shakes his head, checking the rear-view mirror. 'I've got to pull over as well. If he decides to come after us he'll easily catch us. And we've done nothing wrong.'

I'm not at all sure about the wisdom of this, but slowly, all three cars come to a halt. We crane our necks to look behind.

Hale gets out slowly and stretches, one thumb hooked in his belt, the other on the handle of his taser. He saunters up to the driver's window of the other car.

'What if they kill him?' I whisper.

'I don't think they'd dare,' Pedro says, not sounding as confident as I'd like. 'He's on Sherman's side now, anyway. So I heard.'

We wait for what feels like hours but is probably only about five minutes, as Hale stands there having a conversation with the occupants. None of us can make out what's being said. He finally steps back and we all watch in astonishment as the goon car does a slow three-point turn and drives off back towards Tremorglade.

Hale strides over to us and Pedro winds the window down.

'You kids okay?' he asks.

'Yeah,' Pedro says shakily. 'But listen, those guys—'

'I know.' Hale glances at the red lights disappearing into the night. 'I know who they are. I told them they'd be in trouble with Sherman unless they turned back around. I'm lucky they listened.'

'Lucky? You should have arrested them!' Elena says, indignant. 'It's your job!'

He gazes levelly at her. 'How? I've got one taser and one measly set of handcuffs here. No back-up. Police out in Hastaville have got their own problems. This town doesn't belong to us anymore.'

'So you *are* working for Sherman,' I say.

Hale's gaze follows the receding red lights of the car, unable to meet my eye. 'That's what he thinks. But I'm not.'

'Oh? So you're like, not really on their side?' Elena's voice is full of scorn. 'Because from where I'm sitting it's hard to tell the difference.'

He finally turns back to the car. 'I know you don't think much of me, but I'm staying, to do what I can, for the people who're still here. I could leave, you know. But I won't.'

Elena makes a dismissive noise. 'Or maybe you fit right in. Come on, Pedro, let's get out of here.'

'Just a second,' I tell Pedro, and turn back to Hale. 'Then do me one favour. Go tell Amy and Bernice they should get out now, too, with all the Juniper kids, including Ingrid. You have to convince them to go right away.'

'I don't think they'll—'

'You persuade them!' I shout, thumping the sill of the open window. Pedro looks round in surprise.

Hale hesitates, startled, then gives a single nod, silent, before heading back to his car.

As we set off again towards Hastaville, and Sergeant Trash disappears in the rear-view mirror, none of us says a word. Pedro eventually puts the radio on. It tells us Ripper Cultists have clashed with Immutables in Hastaville, luckily on the other edge of town from our hotel, but still too close for comfort.

We're alive. But it feels like defeat.

Passing from the forest that surrounds Tremorglade and out into the open, an unpleasant sensation creeps up on me, the hairs on my neck prickling. I sit up in the back seat, and a flash of white catches my eye, stark among the darkness at the edge of the treeline to my left. It's half hidden, but I think it's a person. Another Alliance goon? A hitchhiker? Why would they be dressed in white, and just standing in the middle of nowhere, all alone? I crane as Pedro speeds past, but whoever it is has sunk back among the trees. Disappeared.

'Did you see that?' I ask Elena.

'See what?'

I turn back around, uncomfortable. 'Nothing, I guess.'

By the time we arrive in Hastaville, bitter winds and horizontal rain are lashing against the car, which groans and judders on two flat tyres as Pedro looks for a parking space near the hotel we've got booked for the night. Mum is coming to meet us here tomorrow evening.

I chuck my bag onto the floor, raising a cloud of dust in the tiny room I've got to myself tonight, then throw myself onto the bed, exhausted, just needing a few minutes to rest before I change into my PJs.

The next thing I know, there's a knock at the door. I stare blearily at the time. It's 4 a.m. Gingerly, I look through the peephole. It's the hotel receptionist. When I open the door, he scowls at me.

'Urgent phone message for you,' he says, handing me a torn scrap of paper with writing scrawled on it, and thumping off back down the stairs.

Why's Mum called the hotel instead of my mobile? Why at 4 a.m.?

But it's not Mum.

> *We met at the lab. I have something you*
> *want. The Moon Inn, Lenton Barr, in the Pyric*
> *Hills. Come quickly.*

Owen.

My heart speeds up. How he knows that I'm here right now, I can't tell.

There's only one thing he has that I want. And if I brought her back, it would change everything.

I know what I have to do.

CHAPTER 12

Ingrid

Sunday 10 February

I had to sneak out early in the morning. Late last night, Bernice knocked on all our bedroom doors and said there'd been a change of plan: we were leaving at first light, packed into the new minibus. I hadn't noticed, but it turns out some of our neighbours quietly slipped away yesterday, having been spooked by the increasingly anti-Ripper messages flying around, and the waves of property destruction in town.

But what clinched it, apparently, was Sergeant Hale coming round. He told Bernice and Amy they shouldn't wait to get out of Tremorglade, because Sherman's out of control and anyone who hasn't openly expressed support for him is in danger. Juniper House is high on their list because of me, because I'm Sel's friend. I'm not sure what to think about Hale. Those Alliance guys said he was working for Sherman, now, but Bernice said he seemed genuinely worried for us.

Either way, the change of plan meant I had a problem.

So before dawn, I left Juniper House, and skulked around the back of the Wellness Centre out of sight, freezing my toes off.

They've gone now, without me. I feel bad because I know they will be distraught, but they have the other kids to think about. Leaving without me was the right thing to do, and that's why I knew they'd do it.

So now I'll just have to find my own way out. With Ben.

When I round the corner of the cul-de-sac, just after 9 a.m., I almost lose my nerve. Sherman's van is parked at the kerb as usual, with Alliance stickers all over it. Several people are unloading huge sacks from the back, heaving them into Sherman's house. I can't read the label from here but I recognize the symbol for toxic chemicals. What are those for?

But I have more immediate concerns. Two goons wearing balaclavas are standing either side of the front door, arms crossed, watching as the last bag is hauled inside the house. One sees me and nudges the other.

Throat dry, I force my feet towards them. I glance up at Ben's window. The curtains stare blankly back.

Just as I approach the door, one of the men slides across to stand in front of it. 'Get lost.'

'I need to see Sherman.'

'Mr Goss said you're not welcome here. We know who you are.'

'He'll want to hear this.'

The two balaclavas glance at each other, and one nods. The other one grabs the front of my coat and yanks me towards him, leans close. His breath is warm and stale on my nose. 'Why haven't you left? Your friends had the right idea. You're no use here.' He lets go and shoves me backwards so I land on my back, hard. Only luck stops my head smacking the pavement.

But I can't give in.

I push myself to sit up. 'But I am. I have information that will be helpful to Sherman. Trust me, he'll be interested.'

'You don't interest me,' says a voice from behind them, where the door has opened.

Sherman emerges onto the step, squinting against the winter sun.

He sneers. 'That's the thing about you people. You all think you're so special. You're not. You're boring. *Boring*. Mindless hounds exchanging fleas and screeching at the moon.'

It's now or never. 'I feel the same. The others have abandoned me. I don't want to Turn anymore. I've had enough.'

He laughs, seeming genuinely amused. 'You've suddenly seen the light? You must think I was born yesterday.'

'It's true,' I insist. 'And it wasn't sudden. Ben knows I've wanted to stop Turning for a while. I told him weeks ago.' I can't help but glance up at the window above me.

The humour drops from Sherman's face. 'Keep my son's name out of your mouth. You will stay away from this house. Away from Tremorglade, like your friends, if you have any sense.'

'I'm telling the truth. Ask Ben.'

'My son is not in his right mind. And that's because of the likes of you. Now leave, before I do something I regret.'

He turns to go back inside. The two goons step forward threateningly. I scrabble to my feet, and shout in haste after him.

'I want to tell you the truth about Sel Archer,' I say. 'Because you're right.'

The door stops closing. Through the scant gap, only shadows. I can't see him, but I know he's there.

I take a breath.

'He's been lying this whole time.'

CHAPTER 13

Sel

'This is the worst idea you've ever had.'

How Elena knew to come and check on me I have no idea. She's meant to be asleep in the room next door, but she woke up when Pedro went out for an early run, like he always does when he's stressed out. So she came knocking for me and caught me getting ready to leave the hotel.

I ignore her and carry on going through my bag, considering what I'll need, what I definitely won't. I left most of my stuff behind, since Mum said she would arrange to ship it out to Greenvale, but I have one change of clothes, a bunch of snacks, my phone and a charging cable. Though I doubt there'll be many places to plug it in where I'm going.

According to my map app, to get to Lenton Barr, I have to go to Mowbury. It's at the end of the train line – there *is* a road that goes a long way around the hills and then cuts into Lenton Barr from the opposite direction, but it's not like I have a car anyway. The train is direct to Mowbury, then Lenton Barr is a few miles away. I guess I'll have to walk or hitchhike there.

It looks tiny on the map. At least it shouldn't be hard to find the Moon Inn, and Owen. When I searched for Pyric Hills, a few recent news articles came up. In the past few days, there've been some nasty attacks in the area – apparently a group of outlaws rampaging around, leaving a trail of devastation behind them. Perfect.

I flex my fingers thoughtfully. My hands look weak, puny. The skin there is pale and translucent, blue-green veins discernible just below the surface. My arms are thin, not a lot of visible muscle. Last year, when I was changing for PE, Leo Wilson grabbed my upper arm and showed everyone how he could squeeze his whole hand round it, finger and thumb touching. I started wearing my jumper over the PE vest after that, and slowly boiled in my own sweat.

Now, if Leo grabbed my arm, he'd get more than he bargained for. Out in Mowbury, there might be far worse than him. But I'm not defenceless anymore.

And what about Owen?

I've been considering him, trying to figure out what he's up to. Why did he steal Barb in the first place? In the lab, I got the impression he felt Gerry wasn't using Barb's full potential. So has he gone somewhere to conduct his own tests? Is he planning to make his own cure? Or do something awful? If he regrets taking her, why wouldn't he just give her back to the authorities? Because he's scared of being arrested?

Which brings me to the big question: why *me*?

Somehow, I have to persuade him to hand Barb over. She is the closest thing to a cure the world has right now. Not that I'm especially in love with the world, these days. Even my home town has rejected me. But Ingrid wants the cure and Ben *needs* it. I feel responsible for both of them.

Also, by rescuing Barb, I can prove that I'm not who all those conspiracy theorists say I am. I can prove I don't have some secret agenda to make everyone Turn, that I'll even help them get rid of their inner Ripper if that's what they want. Maybe then they'll leave me – and my friends – alone.

I explain all this to Elena.

She scoffs. 'You're delusional. Even if that thing is still alive, there's no way this guy is just going to hand it over to you. And you've seen what's going on out in those hills. You'll probably get attacked before you even get close. It's dangerous.'

'Yeah. Well, so am I, apparently.'

'Stop it, you know that's not true. This might actually kill your mum,' Elena tries.

'She'll be fine. She probably won't even be that surprised, after everything else I've done.'

'I'm going to call Pedro right now and tell him,' she threatens. 'He won't let you go.'

'That's why I'm not waiting till he gets back.'

Elena lets out a long, loud cry of frustration and mimes strangling me. 'How can you not see, this is a totally doomed plan?'

I heft my rucksack on my back, tighten the straps.

'Do you even have any money?'

I hesitate. There are a few coins and a couple of notes in my wallet. Mum has my cards. 'Can I borrow some from you?'

'Thought so,' she says, folding her arms smugly. 'So how do you plan to get the train out to Mowbury? You'll need a ticket.'

'I'll sneak on,' I say, with more confidence than I feel. I don't exactly have a lot of experience with public transport. My heroic mission is already throwing up unanticipated problems, and I haven't even left Hastaville.

She growls in frustration, through gritted teeth. 'Just wait here while I get my bag.'

I brighten. 'You're going to lend me some money?'

'No way. I told you: you have zero chance of doing this on your own, you're basically chaos. So I'll have to come with you, won't I?'

CHAPTER 14

Ingrid

Sherman and Ben's house is pretty average for Tremorglade – a medium-sized terraced house with a small garden out the back, two floors, and a basement. A lot of houses here have a basement. Useful for Ripper cages, in the days we needed them. As we pass a door standing ajar in the hallway, one of the Alliance people thuds in from outside holding another of the sacks.

'I can take it down for you, boss?' she offers.

'How many times do I have to tell you?' Sherman retorts. 'The basement is out of bounds. And so is the rest of the house, unless I give you permission. Is that clear? Just leave it here.'

She nods, and scurries out of the front door after dumping the sack. It's got some words written on the other side that I can't read from here.

I glance back at the open door to the basement. I wonder if Sherman will put Ben down there in a cage on Howl night. Maybe he already has. Sherman sees me looking and kicks the door shut.

'This isn't a tour.'

He leads me through to the living room, and directs me to sit down. I go to sit on the closest chair.

'Not there. There.' He points at a sofa.

Whatever. I obey. The room is sparsely decorated, no photographs on the wall, plain furniture, neat. There's no personality to it, and certainly no sign of Ben. The sofa I'm sitting on is firm to the point of being uncomfortable, covered in an itchy, rough fabric, cushionless. It's not a sofa for cuddling up on.

He tells me to wait, then leaves the room. I hear him heft the bag, and his footsteps taking it down the basement steps. Then he's back in the room.

'This is nice,' I say, trying to sound like I mean it.

He sits opposite me, crosses his arms. 'What did you want to say? Make it quick.'

I go for it. 'Listen, I know it's hard to believe. But it's like a lightbulb's switched on in my head. I've been looking at your channel, and the people on it are making sense.' His brow creases marginally, like doubt is creeping in. I push on. 'I hate Turning. I'm sick of it. I want to help your campaign, and especial—' I've been talking too fast, forgetting to take a breath, and my throat closes convulsively in the middle of the word. 'Especially Ben. I want to help Ben, after what Sel did to him. I'm sorry.'

I need to shut up, I'm talking too much, but he's not giving me anything back.

'Even if I believed you, how do you think you can help my son? It's too late for him. Sel made sure of that.'

'Well, I can't stop Ben from Turning, that's true. But I thought it would be good for him to talk to someone about it, someone who knows how it feels. Ben and I are friends, and since his first time is coming up—'

'Yes, I'm aware that you were spending time with Ben behind my back. Against my specific instructions. It's how he ended up in this mess.'

The heat is back in his tone. I need him to calm down. 'Yeah. But it's how I can make things right, too – okay, not *right*,' I add, pre-empting his objection, 'but ... make amends as much as I can. Do something positive.'

He takes a deep breath, narrows his eyes. 'And you say Sel has been lying this whole time. You know what he's been up to?'

'Yes, and—'

He stands up abruptly, and I flinch.

'Tea,' he says. 'Milk and sugar?'

I blink at him, thrown off balance. 'Uh. Milk. No sugar.'

He nods. 'Back in a sec.'

I hear him moving around in the kitchen, the clink of a spoon against china, cupboard doors opening and closing.

I lick my dry lips. Am I getting somewhere? It feels like I'm getting somewhere.

Then Sherman fills the doorway, bringing two mugs of tea. His hands dwarf the delicate mugs, and I half-expect him to crush them. Instead, he passes one to me, puts his own on the shelf behind his chair. Then he goes over to another corner and turns on a lamp. 'Bit dark in here,' he says.

Finally, he sits back down. He sips his tea, staring hard at me the whole time, saying nothing. I take a sip, too. I read once that mirroring someone's body language makes them trust you more. I try a smile, which he doesn't return. Guess he didn't read the same article as me.

A voice inside my head is telling me this is a mistake, that I should get out right now.

Sherman regards me steadily. 'So. You say you want to apologize. I want to hear it. Go ahead.'

I'm pretty sure I already said it, but I oblige. 'Yes, I'm sorry, and—'

'Louder.'

So he wants to humiliate me. Fine. I do my best not to speak through gritted teeth.

'I'm sorry,' I repeat, as clearly as I can.

He scoffs. 'Just like that.' He settles back in the chair, relaxed, smug. Knowing this is his territory and he holds the power. 'All right. Tell me about Sel. He's been lying this whole time, you say?'

I lean back too, trying to mirror him again. 'He fooled us all,' I say, dropping my gaze, trying to look ashamed. 'Especially me. I thought he was my friend, but he was just using me all this time. I can't believe I didn't see it. He must have been behind the whole Sequest business in the first place, like you've been saying for ages.'

Sherman takes another sip of tea.

'So you have evidence that he's involved in this conspiracy? The plan to inflict this disease on *all* of us? Evidence that he is, in fact, now the controlling force behind what used to be Sequest but is currently operating underground?'

When he says 'underground' I *think* he just means 'secretly'. But I can't be sure. I've read some of those wilder theories that Sel's got an actual lair under the mountains. It's hard to tell just how far Sherman's mind has gone.

'Well, it's not so much evidence as stuff I've heard him say. I mean, he didn't keep papers around or anything.' I'm making it up as I go along, now. 'He's too clever for that. But I did once hear him on the phone, saying "We can do it to all of them, even the Immutables now. This new strain is perfect." I don't know who he was talking to, but as soon as he knew I was there, he ended the call. I thought he was messing around, but now I guess it was real.'

Honestly, I know I sound ridiculous. No one in their right mind would believe this stuff, but Sherman seems to be lapping it all up. He's nodding intently. Behind him, in the hallway, the closed door to the basement. What is going on down there?

'This is really helpful, Ingrid. I want to thank you for your bravery.' He comes to crouch in front of me, reaches out and takes my hand. It's clammy. I want to throw up.

'It's, uh, no problem.'

Is this actually working?

Over the next couple of days, I'll keep up the act, and then he'll let me see Ben. Maybe Sherman's already told him Sel and the others have left Tremorglade. Right now, I just want Ben to know I'm here. Then, at the very least, he'll know he's not been forgotten. Sherman won't leave us alone, at first, but there's bound to be a chance before long for me to discreetly help him escape without Sherman realizing. We'll lie low, and look for a chance to leave.

Maybe someone kind can smuggle us out. Failing any other ideas, we'll head through the forest.

My plan is not exactly foolproof. But Sherman's the kind of guy who loves being told he's right, who enjoys people grovelling to him. That's what I'm banking on – that he'll let his guard down.

He sighs. 'It's just a shame it's come too late for Ben.'

My skin goes cold. 'Wh … what do you mean?'

'He's gone, Ingrid.'

Bile rises into my throat. What has Sherman done? Surely he hasn't … not his own son.

'Ben ran away last night. He stole money. I have people

out looking for him, but there's no sign. If only you'd come forward earlier, he might have been saved from making such a foolish choice.'

I can't believe what I'm hearing. 'Ben's left Tremorglade?'

He nods, and huffs out a breath, suddenly overcome with emotion. His face reddens, and his head drops so I can see the top of his buzzcut. I think he might be about to cry. It's so bizarre, I don't know how to respond.

My mind is racing. If Ben is gone, I can go, too. I can leave right now.

His hand is still gripping mine.

'Maybe I could help,' I say, trying not to sound desperate. 'If you know which way he might have gone, I'll get out there and join the search. I want to help.'

He looks up into my face. 'No need. You already have, Ingrid. You already have.' He finally lets go of my hand and turns away, walks back across the room and picks up something from a shelf behind his chair.

It's his phone. I never noticed it before. He must have propped it up there quietly when he brought in the tea.

'What have you got there?' I say, my throat dry.

'Your confession.'

Suddenly it's so obvious I don't know how I didn't realize right away. The lighting. Making me speak louder. He wasn't humiliating or intimidating me, at least not primarily. He was recording.

'I didn't want to make you do it twice. It must have

been hard for you. But once we get it out there, online, it'll bring Ben back faster than anything I can do. And it'll help stop Sel.'

I can't speak. All my effort is going into keeping a neutral expression.

'Don't worry. Sel thinks no one can stop him spreading his disease, but he's wrong. The fightback started in earnest two weeks ago, and now it's unstoppable. This morning, I've had my Alliance set up a roadblock to stop any agitators returning to Tremorglade. I'm keeping us all safe.' A sly look in his eye. 'Soon, everyone will be back to normal, I promise.'

CHAPTER 15

Sel

The train finally drops us at Mowbury around midday. I thought Tremorglade was cold, but out here it feels like the temperature's dropped at least ten degrees. There's thick snow on the ground, a few flakes falling from dense clouds above us. I immediately wonder if we've made a mistake, assuming we could just pop over the hills to Lenton Barr. It's not going to be straightforward. The terrain looks rough. The nearest hills are steep as walls, the sky a grey lid. It's like being in an ice box.

It's hard to understand why anyone decided this dump was worth a train station. What you might call a one-horse town, except the only animals are plump rats, a couple of stray dogs, the occasional fox. Rubbish is strewn across the one street, three crows bickering noisily over some unidentifiable slop in the gutter. There's a grocery store, where we pick up a few supplies, mainly packets of crisps and nuts, since there's not a huge choice. Other than that, almost everywhere is closed and boarded up.

The only other sign of life is a tiny eatery that sells a weird mix of dubious-looking deli meats, a few limp, wrinkled vegetables, and tough-looking pastries. The woman behind the counter wears a uniform streaked with brownish-red stains that might be ketchup or might be related to the filthy bandage on her hand. She hands over a greyish, damp-looking veggie pie for Elena, then starts sulkily putting together a hot dog for me, with an air of having been massively inconvenienced.

'Where is everyone?' Elena asks.

She grunts. I can't tell if it means she doesn't know, or doesn't care. When we ask her the best way to get to Lenton Barr, she stares like we've lost our minds.

'The best way? Run in the opposite direction.'

Elena turns on her sunniest smile. 'We're meeting someone there.'

'At Lenton Barr?' Her entire face crinkles in bemusement. 'You've had a wasted journey, then. Been pranked.'

My heart drops. 'Pranked? It does still exist, right?'

'Oh, it exists, more's the pity. Bunch of weirdos and cranks. I stay well away. More to the point, you'll never make it.'

The woman's gaze slides to me, speculatively. I

recognize the look – I get it a lot outside Tremorglade. People who know they've seen me somewhere but can't quite place me. It takes a while, sometimes, before it clicks.

'If your friend was stupid enough to go out that way recently, I'd say good riddance to bad rubbish.'

I clamp my jaw and watch a fly crawling up the wall behind her, trying to hide my growing impatience.

Elena nods calmly. 'Well, the thing is, he's family. A cousin. So we've been sent to bring him home. Could we get a bus or a cab out there?'

The woman laughs out loud at that. 'What do you think this is, Hastaville? City kids.' She almost spits the last words. 'No road. There's a path, but barely.'

'I guess we'll walk, then,' Elena says, still scrupulously polite. 'Do you have a map we can borrow? Only our phone batteries seem to be draining faster in this cold weather.'

I check mine. She's right. I hadn't noticed. I'm so used to relying on my phone for stuff like this. Trust Elena to think of it.

The woman plants her hands on her hips. 'You're not seriously going out there?'

'We have to. We're worried about our cousin.'

The woman's eyes narrow. 'You should be. If he's been wandering around out there recently, he ain't coming home. Don't you get the news where you're from?'

'We heard about the raiders in this area. Are they still around, then?'

She doesn't answer immediately, shaking her head as she scatters what looks like brown dust from a packet over my hot dog. Then she mutters, 'Seen 'em in the distance. Strange looking. Running all together, like a pack of animals. It was around when Barney went missing. They ate him, I reckon. Never found no trace, but I've seen their leavings, before. Fur. Insides.'

'Barney is your ...'

'Cat.'

'I'm sorry,' Elena says. 'That must be awful. But cats do go missing sometimes ...'

'It's the raiders. Foreigners, no doubt,' she says with distaste, then focuses on me. 'But I suppose it's not just foreigners that behave like beasts.' She pointedly looks at me.

Ah. So she's finally recognized me. And like everyone else, she believes the worst of what she hears.

She's getting on my nerves. Time is ticking. 'So. A map. Do you have one or not?'

She folds her arms. 'My, my, somebody left his manners at home.' To Elena, she says, 'You seem like a nice girl. I wouldn't hang around with this one, if I were you.' She jerks her head in my direction. 'Saw he's been up to some things. He was in the newspaper and on the telly.' The woman turns back to me.

'Oh, that thing at school? That was all a misunderstanding,' Elena assures her. 'It wasn't how it looked.'

'He Ripped out, or bits of him did. Twice. Outside of a full moon. Then he attacked that poor caretaker what was just defending his kid. You want to watch out. He'll bite you soon as look at you. Give you that *monstrum* bug, like the TV lady said.'

'Honestly, he's completely safe, aren't you, Sel?'

I don't answer. It's the *poor caretaker* that finally makes my patience snap. She's just like those anonymous trolls on Facts Unleashed.

'Sel?' prompts Elena.

I'm so tired of this. Of being hated by people who don't even know me. My anger is right here, ready. But I don't feel out of control. It feels right. Solid. Cold.

My mouth tingles with energy, my gums burning. My lips draw back, and I show the woman my teeth. I'm not sure if right now they're my pointy Ripper ones, or just my usual neat, brace-straightened ones, blunt and human. But from the way her smug face drops, I'm guessing it doesn't look like a friendly smile. Good.

'No, you're right. Could happen any time, especially if I feel threatened. Or if someone gets on my nerves.' I lean forward slowly towards her, drawing in her scent. She rears back, and I can hear the blood pumping faster through her arteries. I spread my fingers across the counter. My fingertips buzz. I press them into the surface, hard. Then I meet her eyes. Her pupils are dilated in fear. 'So let's try again. Do you have a map?' My voice is quiet, with a distinct snarl that rolls around my throat. Just behind my shoulder, I hear an intake of breath from Elena, but I don't care.

The woman's jowls wobble as she swallows compulsively, recalibrating her situation. Self-preservation wins out. 'You know what, maybe there is one round here someplace.' She bends under the counter and comes back up with a tattered booklet. I take my hands off the counter. There are tiny gouges in the surface that I don't think were there before. Oops.

I'm aware of Elena's disapproval, but she stays quiet. Probably figures it's too late to backtrack and head down the polite route now.

The booklet is some kind of tourist thing with a fold-out map on the central pages. It looks about a thousand years old, which is presumably the last time this place had any tourists.

Elena thanks her politely, pocketing the map. 'Sorry about my friend being grumpy. He's just worried about our cousin. I hope he's not so rude to people at Lenton Barr.' She glares at me meaningfully, and heads for the door. I trail after her.

As Elena steps out into the cold, the woman calls after us. 'I wouldn't worry. They do normally hate strangers. But *him*? Oh, they'll be big fans.'

The glass in the door shudders as I slam it shut after us. Elena rounds on me.

'What was that?'

'I know, right! What a witch.'

'Not her. You. All that …' She grabs my arm and briefly leans into my face, glaring exaggeratedly, before I shake her off, a touch roughly. 'Menacing. It's just … not like you.'

'There's only one way to get anywhere with people like that. I'm sick to death of conspiracy theorists.'

I expect her to argue, but for once, she doesn't pursue it. I'm glad. I don't want to quarrel with her. She's got a point – it's not like me. The old me, at least. But the old me wouldn't have got us the map.

We eat a little way up the road, sitting on a wobbly wooden bench, while a couple of the crows we saw earlier keep an impatient eye on us, hoping we'll leave crumbs. It's weirdly discomfiting.

'They're kind of creepy, don't you think?' I say, nodding towards the birds.

'They eat meat, among other things, you know,' Elena says conversationally. 'And dead things. A bit like vultures. I've heard they can tell when animals are ill and dying. They won't attack something big, but they'll hang around and wait if they think it's close to death.'

I shiver. 'Gross.'

Elena shrugs. 'They're just trying to survive, same as us. Not a load of choice for food this time of year, I guess.'

I know how they feel. The hot dog is just as grim as it looks – grey, gristly and barely warm inside stale bread that falls apart in my hands – and sits in my stomach like a stone. Elena grimaces as she chews her pie. I give it a fifty-fifty chance we'll be seeing both meals again within the hour.

Elena peruses the map while I look over her shoulder. There might not be a road, but there's a path, though it's a chaotic-looking one, with countless squiggles and bends and none of it a straight line. I'm guessing that's because of all the hills. I feel tired just at the idea of it, but Lenton Barr doesn't look *that* far. We ought to make it by tonight.

A nasty thought strikes me. 'What she said about the raiders. You don't think ... they might have Frozen Fever? Could Owen have set Barb loose already? Gerry said infected people get aggressive. And she said the raiders looked weird. Like a pack of animals.'

Elena wrinkles her nose sceptically. 'There were raiders around well before Barb got out. And she said they looked *foreign*. Not frozen.'

'But she admitted she didn't get a good look.'

'Well, there's no point wondering. Let's assume not and stick to the plan.'

She seems totally calm. I'm glad she's here, even if it should have been Ingrid. Elena is my friend, though we don't have the connection we once had – she still hasn't started Turning, let alone not having the challenges of *extra pilori*. Sitting here with her now, I'm reminded that we go so much further back than that. She might be annoying sometimes but she's on my side, and she's got guts.

Just then, the crows take off in a hurry, cawing, as a fox pokes its head round the corner. It sniffs the air towards us. I stand up to shoo it away and she grabs my arm. 'Woah, steady.'

'I'm fine,' I tell her, trying not to sound grumpy. Ingrid must have told her not to let me chase anything. 'I wasn't going to go after it. Just getting rid of it so we can eat in peace. It's not all the time, you know, that feeling.'

'Are you getting any of those signs right now? Like, heightened senses?'

'Yeah, you smell pretty special.'

'Ha ha.'

'No, I'm serious. It's like you rolled in wolf poop. Guessing you didn't take a shower this morning.'

'Well, someone forced us to leave in a hurry.' She settles back and lets go of my arm.

I change the subject. 'What did you make of what she said about the people in Lenton Barr being big fans of mine?'

'Dunno. I couldn't tell if she was being sarcastic or not. Could go either way. Either they're big on Facts Unleashed, or they're Ripper Cultists, I reckon.'

I groan. 'Ugh, Ripper Cultists. Those people are so weird about me.'

She snorts. 'Yeah, you really hate it when they worship

you. Personally, I'm all for it if they put us in soft beds and give us sacrificial offerings of hot meals. Maybe I'll even let on I'm an original Tremorglade escapee, too. Get some of that hero-worship you've been grabbing all for yourself.'

I know she's only teasing, but it kind of hurts when my friends act like I've got this massive ego and I made my videos for the fame, instead of to be helpful. So what if I enjoy it when people are nice to me – what's wrong with that? Makes a change from being hated.

I take a last glance at my phone. There's a notification from Facts Unleashed about some new video. I'm about to dismiss it, then I notice the title. *BREAKING NEWS: Sel's closest friend says–* My heart thuds, and I click on it to see the whole thing. Painfully slowly, it starts downloading. It's going to take for ever with the signal round here, so I leave it going and stick it in my pocket. I should turn it off, I know, and save battery, but now I can't. It must be about Ingrid. What's she said? Probably something Sherman made up, but still.

Oh, Ingrid. You didn't tell him you're extra *too, did you?*

Elena finishes her pie and washes the taste out with a swig from her water bottle. 'Let's go.'

We make our way towards the path. Starting the ascent into the hills, we walk by what looks at first like a black-leaved tree, but as we pass, the leaves stir and caw; it's a flock of crows, dozens of them sitting among the bare branches. We continue, and after a few minutes, they fly over us all together in a dark cloud, far above, settling on slopes a little way ahead, as though waiting. They're hanging out with us.

Or maybe we look like fresh meat.

CHAPTER 16

The path out towards the hills is barely more than a track, and the thick snow means it's hard to make out, at times. If we can follow it, Lenton Barr should be walkable well before nightfall. Very quickly, though, I regret my choice of footwear, envying Elena's habit of wearing boots for all occasions. Within five minutes, my trainers are sodden.

We're both on edge, constantly looking over our shoulders and straining our ears for the sound of approaching raiders, but we see no one all afternoon. There's only the constant presence of soaring black dots high above us. The sky sends down endless flurries of snow, and gusts of wind blow it into our eyes and mouths, so we don't talk much. The landscape is a mixture of scrubby grass, rocks and deep snowdrifts, a few smallish hills here and there, and some larger ones in the distance ahead, where the path winds between them. Lenton Barr should be nestled on the other side.

I was right about the food. Half an hour into the walk,

our stomachs forcibly rejected it, within minutes of each other. Luckily, once it's out, there are no more ill effects. In a couple of hours we're hungry again.

We're in a narrow valley at the base of two hills, and the wind whips along it brutally. Elena wants to update Pedro on our situation but there's been no signal since we left Mowbury. Now I think of it, I remember reading something in my research last night, about how, early in the Rippocalypse, there were attacks on phone masts in this area – not the raiders, but locals who believed that this is how the *corpus pilori* virus originally spread. That it was carried on phone signals. They destroyed as many as they could, in the hope it would stop them Turning.

Our route takes us up and down and around and my thighs start to protest. A rocky outcrop offers some meagre shelter from the snow, and we share a packet of flatbreads. 'Should've just had these in the first place,' Elena points out, helpfully.

She wanders off round the corner for a toilet break and I check my phone, supposedly to compare the printed map to our location to see what progress we've made, but the first thing I check is the download. It's nearly done, but not quite. I bite my lip in frustration. I've barely got any battery left.

I quickly check my map app. We do seem to be on the right track, and I reckon we have another couple of hours to go before Lenton Barr, which would get us there by dark.

It doesn't really matter what it's like. We just need a place to stay the night, and to be left alone.

Once, soon after the Rippocalypse, I got cornered outside school by a couple of Ripper Cultists. They were polite at first, a bit awestruck. They asked me to sign their chests. I said no, and they started clinging to me, begging for my blessing. It actually got pretty scary, because I couldn't get away. It was like they wanted to keep me. Own me. Totally creepy.

If Lenton Barr is full of people like that, it's going to be a problem.

Of course, these days, maybe I'm not so defenceless.

This might be a good time for a little practice.

Checking behind me in case Elena is on her way back, I shrug off my coat, roll up my right sleeve, shivering. Closing my eyes, I try to take myself back to how I felt during the lab raid, and when Sherman was attacking me. I listen for the buzz in my head, focus on my nerve-endings, take a long, slow lungful of the icy air to draw in the scents. I want to see if I can make claws appear on my right hand again.

For a second or two, there's nothing. Then a shiver that's nothing to do with the cold runs down my fingers, the hair follicles tingling. I open my eyes. Elation washes through me as my right-hand fingernails lengthen, harden, sharpen. Then my other hand starts to go, and I'm suddenly unsure if this is such a good idea. A full Rip-out will tear my clothes off – in a snowstorm in the middle of nowhere. On my left hand, the fur is sprouting along the ridge of my knuckles. I squeeze the muscles reflexively and my phone jumps out of my grip. I make a grab for it but it clatters onto the rock. My coat feels tight all the way down both arms now, my face swelling. *No no nonono.*

'Sel?'

The buzzing abruptly stops. I spin round. Elena is standing there frowning at me.

'Everything okay?'

I blink, look down at myself. My hands are back to their usual pale, bony selves. When I rub my face it's all skin.

'Yeah.' I struggle to get my breath back.

She bends down. 'You dropped your phone.'

I take it from her. The screen is smashed, but it's still working. 'I'll turn it off to save battery,' I tell her, and press it off.

Elena is still frowning, and at first I think she's angry with me, but then she says, 'I thought I saw something. A person.'

My breath catches. 'Near?'

'Not really. On that hill over there.' She points at the craggy ground a few hundred metres away, separated from us by a steep drop.

'Just one person?'

'Yeah.'

I scan the area, squinting, trying to make out any

133

movement, but there's nothing. 'Well, could just be a local. Raiders would stick together, wouldn't they? All those news articles talked about gangs. That woman said they were in a pack.'

'I guess.' She bites her lip. 'It was creepy, though. Whoever it was, they were wearing a mask.'

'Like, a balaclava? I mean, it is cold. I wish I had one right now.' I tuck my chin into my coat.

'Not like a balaclava. It was hard to see, but it looked like … sort of …' She shakes her head. 'It was hard to see through the snow. Come on, you better put your phone away before you break it completely.'

I sigh. 'You still have yours, right?'

'Yeah. All three per cent battery and zero bars of it. I've turned it off.'

We trudge onwards, trying to pick up the pace. I'm frustrated about the phone, but at the same time, I feel positive. I'm making progress, getting the hang of *extra*.

We lose the path a few times in the snow, and have to climb up or down steep slopes to get to it again. My trainers, which at first got soaked and squelched loudly every time I took a step, now creak, like the moisture has turned to a block of ice encasing my toes. At first it's painful, then I can't feel them anymore. I wonder how long they can stay that way before it's too late to get the circulation back. People lose their toes and fingers from this kind of weather – they go black and then drop off, dead. Maybe that's what the crows are hoping for; between the two of us, that's forty tasty little snacks.

Up ahead, a couple of them are fighting over something on the path. They flap off as we approach and we see what they were squabbling about: a sad, torn, bloody scrap of fur that looks like it used to be a small creature.

'A rabbit, maybe, or a squirrel,' Elena suggests. 'Probably a fox killed it.'

'Probably,' I say.

We move on. Before long, there's more. Scattered to the side of the path are further scraps of fur, and entrails, strewn across the snowdrifts.

Elena glances at me. 'These are fresh.'

Unease flutters in my stomach. I turn and look behind us, then up the slopes to our sides, and along the path where it disappears round a bend. Snow catches on my eyelashes and I rub it off, blinking. 'Do foxes hunt in packs?'

'I don't think so.'

Casting my eyes over the gruesome display, I think of the shop woman's missing cat.

'Come on,' Elena says, firmly, almost a snap. 'Keep moving.'

I'm starting to think it's going to be tight to get to Lenton Barr before dark, but we can't go back now. There's no sign of a village yet, just more hills every time we crest one. Elena gets the map out again and the wind almost whips it out of her hands. It's impossible to tell where we are on it.

The snow turns to sleet, pricking at our faces like needles. The temperature keeps on dropping, the light disappearing.

Ahead of us, I keep thinking I see someone. But every time, they're different. Once, I think I see a big, flapping coat, a guy lumbering heavily in the snow, hunched over. Another time the shape is much smaller, faster. But each time, I blink and they're gone. I reach out with my sense of smell, but get nothing other than vegetation scents, the occasional fox, and Elena, who *really* needs a shower. My mind is playing tricks.

» » »

Just when I'm starting to think we'll have to camp out here, and probably die of exposure, we round the base of a hill and see lights ahead. They illuminate a scattering of houses and what looks like a single street.

Those lights, few and dim as they are, are the most beautiful sight I've ever seen. I'm so tired, and wet, and cold. I don't even care anymore if the residents want to dress up in robes and chant around me. Heck, they can have a few drops of my blood too if that's the cost of a night's sleep and a hot meal.

As we get closer, I can see there's an eight-foot wire fence that seems to stretch all the way round the village.

Security conscious. Can't say I blame them. But there's a gate up ahead. We trudge towards it.

'Looks like we're in luck,' Elena says. She's turned her phone on to use the torch. I follow its beam to a poster flapping against the fence.

GUIDED MEDITATION

The blessing of Turning

By Howlmaster Bob Quincy

Join us every Tuesday 7 p.m. in the Moon Inn

for a celebration of Ripper beauty and peace!

Ripper Cultists, then. I'll be welcome here. It's just as well – we had no Plan B. We've ditched Mum, and Pedro and Mika, to come up here, when all they were trying to do is get us to safety. I wonder what the old Sel would have made of me now – the Sel whose idea of risk was eating biscuits a day past their best-before date.

'Be nice to these people, okay?' Elena warns. 'I'm sure if you try really hard, you can get even these people to hate you. But we can't afford to go around making enemies.'

'I don't make them, they make themselves,' I mutter.

'It doesn't help if you start threatening people— What's wrong?'

I've stopped dead, and she stumbles into me. We've

reached the gate. It's made of the same metal as the fence, woven into small squares a couple of centimetres across. It's slightly open, swinging back and forth across an area scraped clear of snow. There are large bolts at the top, middle and bottom. A single crow sits atop the steel post, eyeing us curiously.

There's a dark brownish stain all down its length, and I can tell there's a lot more spread around under our feet, beneath the thick snow. It's a few hours old, but the iron reek of it hits the back of my throat powerfully.

'What is it?' Elena stands next to me. I guide her hand to shine the torch beam onto the steel post.

'Blood.'

CHAPTER 17

Pedro

I don't know what I did to deserve this. Chasing around after my sister and her friends is like trying to herd cats.

When Elena and Sel went AWOL early this morning, obviously I would have gone after them if I'd had the first clue where they'd gone. Elena was good enough to leave me a note at the hotel, telling us that they were 'following a lead on Barb', plus a bossy instruction to keep in touch with Ingrid. She stopped sharing her location with me, so I knew she meant it. You can imagine how it went down with Dad and Sel's mum, Jenny, when I had to break it to them. There was no point hanging around in Hastaville, so I sped right over to Greenvale to be with them.

Bernice rang me in a panic, saying Ingrid had gone missing during the night, that they'd had to leave without her. She'd been desperately hoping that Ingrid had made her way out on her own, and was somehow with us, and when I had to disappoint her, she burst into tears.

I'd literally just pulled up in Greenvale, halfway through the day, when Ingrid's video popped up. I instantly knew she was in real trouble. There's no way she did that voluntarily.

Sherman's been out of control for a while. But this is on a new level.

He's obviously kidnapped Ingrid.

That's the only explanation for the video we all saw yesterday. I can't imagine what he must have done to her to make her say that stuff about Sel, but I feel sick to my stomach.

So as evening draws in, I'm driving Dad's car, with new tyres, down the road through the woods, all the way back to Tremorglade, and I don't know what I'll find when I get there. Dad didn't want me to go, obviously, worried though he is for Ingrid. He got on the phone to Hastaville police, and then every force in the region, trying and failing to interest them in what might be going down in Tremorglade. I could have told him it was hopeless. They know they'll face an armed force of Immutables if they come here to intervene. And they know the only way that ends is with a lot of people getting killed. Who wants to kick that off?

It's always down to us. I left while Dad was on hold for the fifth time.

'Are we nearly there yet?'

The voice from the back seat makes me swerve so hard in surprise that I nearly go off the road. The brakes judder as I shove my foot down, and turn to look behind me.

Mika's grinning head pops up. 'You should drive more carefully, Pedro. You nearly crashed then.'

My speechless face, mouth opening and closing and making incoherent noises of outrage, just makes her laugh.

'Come on, you didn't think I was going to let you rescue Ingrid alone, did you? You said you needed a distraction.' She points both index fingers at herself. 'Plus, I've got nunchucks in my bag.'

I should have known. You don't discuss anything in Mika's hearing unless you want her involved. Of course she wouldn't ask anyone if she could come – because they'd say no. Why do I never learn? Of all my sister's wild friends, Mika is the one most likely to jump head first into danger without pausing to think. And considering my sister and her friends, that's saying something.

Finally I get the power of speech back. 'Mika! Dammit, now I have to take you back!'

'You can't. No time. This is urgent. Besides, you need me.'

'It's too dangerous.'

'Excuse me, but who saved us from the Revenant? Remind me.'

'Ben,' I say, stubbornly.

'And ... ?'

Much as I hate to admit it, she has a point. Without her, things would have turned out very differently last year. And I have a feeling that if I drive her all the way back to Greenvale, she'll find another way to get involved – one where I won't be able to keep an eye on her.

'Mika, I swear, you'll be the end of me. The nunchucks stay in the bag. If Sherman's lot see them, we're dead. Okay? In. The. Bag. You're a normal little girl. Cute. Quiet. Maybe a bit scared. Got it?'

'Totally!' she chirrups.

I turn back to the front, and heave a long, heavy sigh. She scrambles into the passenger seat. I start driving again, feeling her annoying little smile at my side.

As the road finally breaks through the trees and reaches the edge of town, I see how far things have moved on, even in the few hours since I left. There's a makeshift roadblock, staffed by six people in camo gear and balaclavas. They're armed. As I drive towards it, they look in my direction, straighten up, and wave me down.

I consider my options. Drive right through the barrier and die in a hail of bullets, or stop.

'Mika, don't say a word, okay? Leave it to me.'

She merely nods, briefly, her face drawn and serious.

My heart thudding fast, I pull over, tilting my baseball cap as low as I can over my eyes without actually covering them.

One of them comes over and makes a winding motion with his hand. I press the button and my window slides down.

'Hey!' I say, aiming for casual, cheerful.

'Turn around. No one comes in, right now. Local emergency.'

He pulls out his phone, swipes and shows me the screen. It's the Facts Unleashed site. *Tremorglade: Emergency Measures in Place.*

'See here? Keep an eye on this site. It's where you'll find all the latest updates, direct from Sherman Goss. He's got this place well in hand.' I glance at the other goons. Several of them appear to be scrolling on their phones. Hanging off Sherman's every word.

I smile weakly. 'Oh, we're big fans of the guy. But our grandma's in there. She needs her meds. We've got them right here.'

He holds out a hand. 'No worries. I'll get them to her.'

Didn't think this one through, did I? I turn to the back seat and make a show of rifling in my bag. Miraculously, there's some painkillers in one of the pockets, in a torn packet. 'Here,' I say.

He takes them, dubiously, turns the packet over, reading it.

Peering past him, I can just see the first shops and houses of Tremorglade at the end of the road. There's no movement. Those who've stayed seem to be lying low. No surprise, with these guys in charge.

'Where does she live?'

'Who?'

His eyes narrow. 'Grandma.'

'Oh, right. She lives at number twenty-six, Fallowfield Rise.' There isn't a number twenty-six, I realize. There are only five houses on the entire road, but I'm guessing he's a newbie, drafted in as a fan of Sherman's, answering a call for backup on Facts Unleashed.

'I'll be sure to drop them round,' he says, with a tone that tells me this conversation is ending. 'Now turn around and go.'

There's a loud snuffle from beside me.

'B-b-but I want to see Granny!' Mika begins to wail, like she's about four years old. I turn and gape at the actual tears suddenly pouring down her cheeks. It's like she just turned on a tap. The guy looks alarmed, glancing back helplessly towards his colleagues, who have their backs to us.

I sense doubt. Weakness. 'We'll only be a few minutes,' I say, 'Mate, can't you just …' I trail off as there's a loud *clunk-clunk* from behind him. He jumps, and moves aside, revealing a senior colleague, who's apparently just chambered a round in his gun.

The others, who've been standing there chatting, hear it and turn towards the car, straightening up.

Mika turns off the tears as abruptly as she turned them on. We both sense that the threat is real.

'Problem here?' the gunman says, narrowing his eyes at me. I angle my face down slightly so he mainly gets a view of my baseball cap – I'm not as famous as Sel, but it's possible he recognizes me.

'We just want to visit my gran.' Mika sniffs.

'Not today. Go back the way you came, if you ever want to see her again.'

I take a look past the men, into town. My engine is still on. My foot is right there, ready to hit the accelerator.

In my favourite movie, *Plague Terror*, the hero, played by Fen Zhao, gets past a whole troop of soldiers to rescue a classroom-full of pre-schoolers, by driving up fast and spinning the car round, taking out all the baddies like skittles, sending them flying in all directions. She gets the stragglers with a couple of martial-arts moves. But I'm no Fen Zhao. Even if I was on my own, I wouldn't. With Mika in the car, there's no question.

I put the car in reverse, do a slow three-point turn, and drive back up the road as carefully as our fictional grandma.

Mika is uncharacteristically quiet.

It's only when they're out of sight that I start punching the dashboard in frustration.

CHAPTER 18

Sel

I scan the view in front of us, wondering how much more blood might have been spilled in the village. Through the gate, a row of brick houses huddles against the blizzard, slightly run down but not dilapidated. Some of them have lights on inside, though there's no sign of anyone around. A handful of vehicles are parked, covered with snow. Considering the villagers cared enough about security to erect the fence, it's odd they've left the gate open, and no one's keeping a lookout. There are no footprints visible, but the snow would have covered any fairly quickly.

Suddenly, the crow on the steel post next to us explodes into flight, cawing loudly, and flaps towards the village. Something spooked it.

Elena draws in a sharp breath. She's looking behind us, back up the path into the hills. 'Did you see that?'

I peer as far as I can in the direction she indicates, but the weather means I can't see clearly more than a few metres ahead.

'Uh-oh. There, too.' Elena points at another angle, up a slope. In between the trees, I see it. Movement. Something black and white. An animal? I train my senses on it but can't make out a human scent other than Elena's.

We're both peering so hard into the distance that we fail to notice the figure approaching until it looms out of the darkness only metres away. Tall, wrapped in a bulky coat, wearing a white mask.

Running towards us, arms outstretched, as though we're long-lost friends.

I grab Elena and haul us both through the gate, slamming the middle bolt across just before the newcomer slams into the wire fence, hard.

It's a woman, or at least it used to be. She bashes her fists against the fence, trying to get to us. They're white as the snow. As she hits the wire repeatedly, her hands are little more than chunks of ice. The knuckles crumble a little, flakes of frost falling to the ground.

Her face, pressed up against the wire squares, is smooth and white like an ice rink, in which her mouth is open, bright red, a gaping wound. Steam billows from it in a cloud. Her eyes are so bloodshot they're scarlet. It looks as though she's screaming, but the only sound that emerges is a kind of elongated exhale, a rasping breath like wind through trees. The thing that shocks me most, somehow, is the smell. Or rather, the lack of it. There's nothing to identify this person as human, or even animal, in her scent. Used as I've become to the cocktail of molecules that everyone sheds, their absence is shocking, repellent. I reel back.

Elena recovers her wits before me, reaching down to slide the bottom bolt across, in between the judders of the woman's barrage. I do the same with the top bolt, flinching away when one of the woman's ice fingers pokes through a wire square next to my face.

'Sel.' Elena draws my attention to the fence further along. The person we saw clambering down the slope has reached it and is clawing at the fence, the metal clanging and juddering. The poster rips into shreds and is whipped away on the wind. This figure is smaller, skinny, a teenager, maybe.

'Is it going to hold them?' I ask Elena as we back away, eyes on the two attackers.

'I think so. It's strong. Besides, look, they're getting bored.'

Bored may be the wrong word for it, but as we've retreated towards the village, the two of them have calmed, slightly. They're still watching, groping at the fence, but no longer flailing themselves into a shower of snowflakes.

Continuing to glance back at them, we trot down the

street. My whole body is still buzzing from the shock of the encounter. There's no doubt in my mind that those are Frozen Fever victims. I knew in theory what the disease did to people, but somehow I never pictured it quite like this.

I glance over at Elena but she's frowning in concentration, trudging through the snow, apparently focused on finding our destination. I can't help but admire her. Her nerves are shredded too, I can tell, but she's keeping it together.

'Look.' Elena points at the largest building, which announces itself on a sign as the Moon Inn. Well, that was simple.

The door opens immediately at my push, and swings wide. We're in a bar area, brightly lit. Several circular tables are dotted around the room, surrounded by chairs, a few fallen over as though roughly shoved aside. Empty and half-drunk glasses dot the counter and tables. The smell of stale beer makes me want to heave.

'Hello?' Elena calls, warily. 'Anyone here?'

I shut the door behind us. We call out a few more times, louder, but there's no reply, no movement. There's a key on the inside of the door, and I turn it for good measure. The silence is complete.

'I'm going upstairs to check,' Elena announces. 'You stay here and keep an eye on those guys.'

I step gingerly across the garish red swirl-patterned

carpet, the faint crunch of crisp crumbs under my melting trainer, and make my way to a cushioned bench under a window. It squeaks as I kneel on it and peer out. There's no sign of our attackers, though I can see only a small section of fence from here.

There's a radiator here, too, and it's warm. I press myself against it.

To my relief, Elena returns after a couple of minutes, clambers onto the bench next to me and cups her hands round her face at the window. 'Looks like they've wandered off.'

My adrenaline is slowly leaking away, my fingers and toes defrosting.

'So ... the blood by the gatepost,' Elena says. 'Theirs?'

I shake my head.

'Could it have been an animal? There's probably bears out here.'

'Human,' I say, without hesitation. 'More than one.'

Elena takes that in. 'So, a bunch of people died up by the gate. Trying to stop something or someone getting in, maybe?'

'If so, clearly, they failed.'

We stay motionless for a few moments, Elena kneeling and staring out the window, keeping watch, me sitting determinedly facing into the room. I lay my palms on the table, feeling the tacky surface, trying to take comfort in its ordinariness.

'Maybe whatever came in, it left again.'

'Maybe,' I agree.

A thud from the windowsill makes us both jump, but it's just a falling icicle. All the same, it takes a minute for my nerves to stop vibrating.

'Well, anyway,' Elena sighs eventually, 'obviously, those things were Frosties.'

'Say what?'

'People with Frozen Fever.'

'Frosties? Did you just make that up?'

'Yes, and?'

'Fair enough. Unless it's just a really bad rash,' I say, trying to keep the lightness going, but I'm not feeling it, and neither is she.

'Sel, you told me that when you were in the lab, and you struggled with Owen, Barb got out of control at one point, right? And then he managed to get her back in the box.'

I nod.

'Could he have been infected right then? How long does it take?'

An image flashes into my brain, Barb slipping down Owen's sleeve. I shrug. 'Dunno. Gerry never got down to that level of detail. I do know she needs to feed a *lot*, though. Every few minutes. Or she'll die.'

'That's why she's a parasite, I suppose. In an ideal world she'd be attached to someone the whole time.'

I try to think back, and suddenly I see it in my mind:

the rucksack. 'Owen left a bag behind, on the floor. I think it had more food in it for her. The balls made with *corpus pilori* blood.'

'But he left it behind? That would mean—'

'Well, maybe there was some in the box with her, too. But not as much as he'd planned on taking. If she ran out of food, she'd die very quickly.'

'But we know she didn't die. So...'

We fall silent for a moment. We both know what this probably means: most likely, Barb got her next meals from Owen himself. Maybe he thought he would just give her a little to keep her alive until he could get more. Or maybe she got out of the box again, ravenous and unstoppable. Either way, he's almost certainly infected. And then he's infected those other poor souls.

I almost feel sorry for him. What a way to find out you're not quite the expert parasite-handler you thought you were. But my sympathy is overtaken by anger at his sheer stupidity and arrogance.

And I can't help but remember Barb was only millimetres away from *me*.

'Whatever Owen wanted to talk to you about,' Elena breaks into my thoughts, 'I don't think he's in a position to chat anymore.'

My shoulders droop. She's right. We came out here to find Owen, but there's no way we're equipped to deal with him if he's turned into one of *them*.

It's one thing to persuade Owen to give me Barb in a box, quite another to *remove* her from him.

'Those poor souls,' Elena says quietly, resting her forehead against the window. 'Do you think there are more? How many could he have infected?'

'No idea.'

I put my head in my hands. We need to think about what to do next, but I'm so tired. At least it's warm in here – the radiator next to us is blasting out heat. My circulation is finally reaching my toes. I wiggle them, trying to get the image of the woman's face out of my head. The fever inside giving her breath the heat of a furnace, while frozen crystals merged over her skin to make á carapace of smooth ice.

If Owen was infected first, he'll be even further gone than that.

Elena finds some packets of nuts behind the bar and we guiltily open them, starving. 'I'll leave some money,' she assures me.

I nod, though neither of us really think the owners of this place will be back for it. Maybe those Frosties out there used to be the owners.

'We'd better knock on some doors, find out what's happened. There have to be *some* people at home.'

After polishing off five packets of nuts between us, there's nothing stopping us getting on with it. But neither of us wants to move. It feels safe in here. We've shut out some of the danger beyond the fence, but we have no idea what might still lurk in the street. I twist in my seat and peer out of the window, checking for movement, but there's none.

Eventually, we drag ourselves to the inn door. I unlock it and we step into the street, looking both ways before leaving the safety of the step.

At least the blizzard has stopped. A streetlight glows dimly above our heads, giving us strange shadows as we crunch across the road to the nearest house with a light on.

Elena raps on the door, then after a few seconds tries again. And again. We move on to another, then another, with a growing sense of unease.

The entire village seems to be empty.

It doesn't take long before we've knocked on every single door, including those without a light on. Nothing has stirred. It's possible that everyone is hiding, but I don't think so. There's an emptiness to this place.

At the opposite end of the village, we walk up to the fence. There's another gate, this one big enough for vehicles, and it's wide open, a road stretching away into the distance, barely visible under a thick layer of snow. Belatedly, I remember from the map that there's a road that goes all the way around the hills to arrive here. I'd forgotten about it because it was no use to us. Cursing ourselves for not thinking of it earlier, we hurry over and close the gate, bolting it.

Eventually, we make our way back to the inn. I've never felt more dejected. Elena insists on remaining positive, as we lock ourselves in again.

'The way I see it, we look around in the morning. We don't know for absolute certain Owen is infected – maybe Barb got loose from him, and attached herself to someone else. If that's what happened, he'll come here, like he said, and we'll find out what he wants. If he doesn't turn up … I guess we go to Greenvale and meet the others. At least we tried.'

I nod. I'm not holding out much hope anymore. It was always a long shot, but a part of me really thought I might come home bearing Barb, and turn everything around. I see now that was stupid.

Sneaking a glance at Elena, I have a feeling she always knew it was. She came because she knew I was going to do it anyway and didn't want me to go alone. She came just because she's my friend.

In all the darkness of our situation, the thought is a tiny pilot flame.

'There's a shower and comfy beds upstairs,' she says. 'We need sleep.' I don't argue, even though she's giving off Goldilocks vibes, and I'm very aware the bears may be coming home any minute. I'm cold, wet and trembling with exhaustion. It's either this or, die of exposure outside.

Elena bounds up the stairs like she's just tapped into a new energy source and starts showing me our options while I trail wearily behind her, listening to her commentary.

'Bathroom – ew, not too clean, but never mind. Bedroom, no bedclothes but fine. Bedroom – with *blankets*! She kicks her boots off, rushes in and dives onto the mattress, wriggling under the covers.

'Hey, you're still wet!' I object.

Her face emerges with an impish grin. 'But it's so lovely and warm under there.'

'This is someone's home. We should treat it with a bit of respect,' I say.

She snorts. 'From the boy who keeps mouldy coffee cups along with pants under his bed.'

I squirm, but brazen it out. 'Yeah, it's *my* bed. That's the—'

Creak.

We both freeze. That came from just down the hallway. The bedroom door is half open, the landing light on outside.

We locked up downstairs, I'm sure we did.

Instantly, my body sings with tension. That wasn't just old-house noise.

Elena slithers off the bed backwards, taking all the covers with her onto the floor on the far side of the bed. I cast around desperately for something to defend myself with.

There's another creak, then another. Faint, but definite.

Someone walking along the landing very slowly, trying not to make a noise.

Creak. A shadow creeps across the swirly carpet in the doorway. *Creak.*

It stops. Silence.

I raise my arms defensively. The prickling of my fingernails tells me *extra* is ready to come out to play. My ears pick up the sound of shaky breathing. An instant later my nostrils flare, a scent trickling in, and my mouth falls open in disbelief. My arms drop to my sides.

And then he's standing in the doorway, and we're all gaping at each other. The tension leaves my body in a rush and my first word comes out as a laugh.

'Ben?'

CHAPTER 19

It seems impossible that Ben is here, but he is, he really is.

Elena throws herself at him with a scream, and we both hug him until he complains we're squeezing him like a tube of toothpaste.

'Where's Ingrid?' I look over his shoulder, expecting to see her grinning in victory at having saved Ben.

But he frowns. 'Isn't she with you?'

The disappointment hits me like a sack of rocks to the chest. 'She stayed to rescue you from that house. From your dad.'

He looks shocked. 'Oh. No. I left on my own. The same night you did.'

'So what happened?'

'I hadn't been planning to get away. I thought eventually I'd get through to him, persuade him that you're not the enemy, that me Turning won't be the end of the world. I know he can be awful, but it's ... complicated. He loves me. He thinks he's protecting me.'

I resist the temptation to catch Elena's eye. We both know what we think of Sherman. But he's not our dad, is he?

'Does Ingrid know you've gone?' I ask.

'I don't know. Maybe, by now?'

'So what made you decide to leave after all?'

'I got a message.' He digs into his coat pocket. 'One of the Alliance guys passed it to me when Dad wasn't looking. I think somebody must have paid him to give it to me. Must have been a lot, given what Dad would have done to him if he'd found out.'

He shifts awkwardly, as though acknowledging his contradictory statements about Sherman, and passes me a piece of paper. It's similar to the note I got at the hotel in Hastaville. An invitation from Owen to come here.

'That's the parasite guy, right? The one that stole it from the lab. I knew Dad wouldn't let me go in a million years, and he'd just storm out there all guns blazing and probably end up getting killed … I'd overheard Dad was about to set up a roadblock to stop people coming in, and I could see from my window that some locals were packing up to leave. When you all left that night, Dad relaxed a bit, and I was allowed out of my bedroom, although he kept my phone. So I waited till he was asleep, then slipped out the back door, over a few fences, and begged a lift out to Hastaville from a couple who didn't know who I was. Told them my parents had accidentally left me behind. Then I got a taxi to Lenton Barr.'

My jaw drops. So he took the long way round. 'You're kidding me. A *taxi*? All the way out here? That must have cost a fortune.'

'No kidding. It took me about twenty tries to find someone who'd even take me, and I had to pay like ten times the normal price per mile, in advance. Even then, he wouldn't go the whole way, after the radio said there were raiders in the area. When he heard that, I had to get out and walk through the blizzard. Luckily we were only a mile away.'

'How did you get that kind of money?' Elena asks.

He bites his lip. 'You know that crowdfunder of Dad's? He's been keeping it as cash, in a drawer in the kitchen. I kind of borrowed it.' He looks deeply uncomfortable. 'I figured the whole point of it was to help get a cure, so once I came back with Barb he'd forgive me.'

I don't like to say it, but I reckon he might be wrong about that.

'So where's Owen?' Ben asks. 'Is he here?'

'Ah. About that,' Elena sighs. 'He might not be coming. It looks like he got infected with Frozen Fever. Some people definitely already have, anyway.'

Ben's face falls as we tell him about the two poor souls we 'met' on our way in.

'You think one of them was Owen?'

I shake my head. 'Neither of the two we saw. I could tell even with the general iciness going on. But if they've got

160

it, they most likely caught it from him. Unless Barb got out of the box and attached to someone else early on.'

'Okay,' Ben says. 'So there's two possibilities. Either he's infected, in which case we really don't want to meet him. Or he's fine, but he doesn't have Barb anymore, in which case he won't meet us because he's got nothing to bargain with.'

Elena nods. 'That's what we figured. So we sleep here tonight, and in the morning, we head out and report to the authorities that Owen is in this area, and that there's an outbreak of Frozen Fever.'

She doesn't point out the obvious: that we'll have to survive the journey first. Could we maybe boost a car? Ben can drive … a little. Although last time he did, it ended with him crashing into a retirement home. And tomorrow night is Howl night – at least when Ben Turns he won't be useless and goofy like a normal Ripper, but it'd surely be better to at least have reached somewhere safe when it happens.

I pull out my phone, in case it has a bar or two so we can call someone. It doesn't. What it does have is two per cent battery, and a fully downloaded video.

I should save that battery. It would be foolish to waste it.

But if Ingrid's in trouble, I need to know.

While the others get settled, deciding we should all sleep in the same room tonight, I casually announce I'm going to the bathroom.

Sitting on the closed toilet lid, I click on the video.

First, I hear Ingrid's voice apologizing. Then the visual loads. She's sitting in a chair I don't recognize, in a room I don't recognize.

Sherman makes her apologize again, and my teeth grind so hard, my jaw hurts. Has he taken her captive?

My heart sinks. She's going to tell him she's got *extra*, like me, despite the fact I *begged* her not to.

But she doesn't say that.

She says something much worse.

CHAPTER 20

Ingrid

When Sherman told me what he'd done, I felt like I was going to puke. I said I needed the bathroom.

Once inside I collapsed onto the toilet lid and now I'm sitting here in shock. Has a plan ever backfired so spectacularly? I thought I was being so clever, and now I might just have put the final nail in Sel's coffin. I feel even sicker when I think about it. Sherman actually seems happy with me. My performance must have been convincing, because he believes I'm genuine. He actually patted me on the back as I scrambled out of the room, and told me I'd been brave. He's uploading it already.

I should make a run for it. Now I know that Ben is gone, there's no reason for me to stay.

Except … there is something very odd going on here. Sherman definitely didn't want me looking in the basement, earlier. Those guards outside the house … they're not his bodyguards. And they're not here to keep watch on Ben, because he's gone. So they must be here to protect something else. The way Sherman said the fightback had begun two weeks ago … That's when things started to go really wrong for Sel. It's when Barb got stolen.

A crazy thought hits me. Could *Barb* be in the basement?

I dismiss the idea right away. Sherman wouldn't have the first clue how to look after her. He's arrogant and stupid but even he surely knows he's not qualified. Taking her would slow down the search for a cure, not speed it up.

But what if he *did* know how to look after her? What if he had expert help? From someone like Owen, the guy who stole her. What if Owen stole her *for Sherman*? Maybe Sherman didn't trust Probius to finish the job of finding a cure, after all?

My mind races. All the threats, the pressure on us to leave … The dead squirrel on Sel's doorstep, too, maybe? Was that just because he's hateful? Or did he want us out of the way for another reason?

What's down there?

Once this is over, I can upload my own video retracting what I said, but right now I'm starting to think I should make the most of my position. Sherman actually thinks I'm on his side.

I need to know what's in the basement.

But when I open the bathroom door, Sherman's standing right there. We go back into the living room, and I keep him talking for a couple of hours, telling him what he wants to hear. As dusk starts to fall, I think he's almost fond of me.

I'm about to ask if I can stay for dinner, hoping there'll be a chance to poke around, when he decides our time is over.

'You should get home.' There's that glance towards the basement again. He wants to get down there.

'How about I make us some food? Bernice and Amy have gone, so I've no one to go home to.'

But he shakes his head. 'Come back tomorrow, if you like. We'll put you on video again. Better quality, with a proper camera. I'm sure you've got more to say.'

He closes the door. I feel the eyes of the two goons on me as I walk down the street.

For sure I'm coming back tomorrow. And this time I'll get what I need. As for how to leave afterwards … for that I'm going to need help.

CHAPTER 21

Sel

'He's got her. He's got her.' I'm hyperventilating. I can't seem to stop. 'What's he done to her?'

'Calm. Breathe, Sel. Breathe.' Elena's hands press on my shoulders.

'He's tortured her.'

Ben is shaking his head. 'No. No, he wouldn't do that.'

'Ben, have you *met* your dad?'

But he's not having it. 'I mean it. He's lost his way, and he's angry, and he intimidates people ...'

'And throws chairs at them,' I put in.

'... but he wouldn't kidnap and torture a teenager. He just wouldn't.'

'What about *only* kidnap, then?' I snap. 'And *threaten* to torture.'

Ben hesitates, just enough to win me the point. 'I don't think—'

'Actually,' Elena says slowly. 'I think she did it willingly. Look at her body language. She said she was staying because she had a plan. I think that was it.'

I laugh hysterically. 'That's ridiculous. How would that ever—'

'Persuade him she's on his side,' Elena presses. 'Get close, so she could rescue Ben. Who, as it turns out, didn't need rescuing.'

I open my mouth to object, but she's right. No wonder Ingrid refused to tell me what she planned.

'But...' I splutter. 'Why would she let him video it? And post it all over the internet?'

'Oh, you're worried about your reputation?'

'It's not that...' I break off. A stab of shame. Maybe it is, a little. But what people think of me is not the immediate problem. 'I'm scared for her.'

'Pedro will be on the case, I promise you. He won't just abandon her.' This mollifies me, a tiny bit.

Ben jumps in. 'I don't think she knew she was being recorded. Did you notice, she wasn't looking at the camera at any point.'

I hadn't noticed that.

'Yeah ... you're right.'

Ben adds, 'Sel, I'm really sorry I left without her. I'm sorry about my dad. I'm just ... sorry.'

His eyes shimmer with tears. I can't imagine what it's like to be the son of someone like Sherman. Love isn't something you can just turn on and off.

I finally breathe out, shakily. 'It's not your fault. I'm sorry if I ever made you feel like it is. And I'm sorry I made things so much worse for you at home.'

He shakes his head. 'That wasn't your fault, either. You saved my life. And if you say this *extra* thing isn't so bad, then maybe I can handle it, too.'

Elena looks sharply at me, but says nothing. She gets up and announces she's going to find us some food downstairs.

When her footsteps fade away, I say to Ben, 'Actually, it has its advantages. Don't tell Elena, because she and Ingrid are weird about it, but I'm learning to control my Rip-outs. You could, too.'

He makes a 'maybe' face, and shrugs. 'Show me, then.'

And for the next few minutes, quietly, I do, growing in confidence as I realize how quickly I've come on even in the past few hours. Ben, on the other hand, struggles to produce so much as a single claw. Early days, I assure him – I used to be exactly the same. Practice, that's the key.

» » »

After an actually pretty okay dinner of pizzas from the inn's freezer, we settle down to sleep in the main bedroom, having dragged in two more mattresses so we can all be together.

None of us immediately feel like sleeping. At first we're alert to any tiny noise – the radiators switching off, water in the pipes – but slowly we relax. Something tells me that if the Frosties try to break in, they won't be subtle about it.

We chat for a while, about our parents, and about how much trouble we'll be in. Ben wins on that score.

Then Elena says, even aside from his dad's reaction, it must be hard for Ben, not being Immutable anymore.

'Dunno, I guess I'll find out tomorrow at dusk. But the idea of it isn't actually so bad. It's something that you guys always had and I didn't. Even though you haven't Turned yet, Elena, you've always known that you *will* eventually. I've often thought it would make me feel more part of our group, you know?'

Elena and I immediately argue that he already is, but he waves our insistence away.

'Yeah, yeah. But, I mean, I *am* kind of nervous about tomorrow night. My first one.'

'Course,' Elena says reassuringly. 'I will be too, whenever mine eventually comes. But we'll get through it. Other people do. And we shouldn't lose hope just yet. Whether we get Barb back or not, I really believe some day soon there'll be a way to help us get better.'

Her phrasing rubs me the wrong way. 'We're not *ill*.'

'Uh, I mean, both *corpus* and *extra pilori* are viruses—'

'But not ones that makes us sick,' I insist. 'You know, some viruses are *beneficial*. They help protect people, make them stronger.'

'Well, Sequest didn't release it to help us. And Harold didn't bite you as a favour.'

'I know that,' I tell her, trying not to sound defensive. 'But Gerry said it's been shown that Turning is good for lots of people, benefits their mental health. And there's aspects of this *extra* upgrade that have helped me, too.'

'Upgrade?' Elena wrinkles her nose. 'Sel, you didn't need upgrading.'

'Er, hello? Who said I was the clumsiest boy in Tremorglade? You and everyone else.'

She sits up. In the moonlight streaming through the window, she looks devastated. 'If I ever made you feel like that, I'm sorry. Really. There was never anything wrong with you before.'

'And now?'

She hesitates. 'It just seems like you have less control, not more.'

'You're wrong. Seriously. I reckon I could even stop myself Ripping out on Howl night, if I tried.' It's a bold claim, and I'm nowhere near as confident as I sound, but I'm doubling down. 'I'm new to it – I just need to work on it.'

'You never used to threaten people. That's new.'

'Maybe I'm just not so willing to put up with being

mistreated anymore. It's not my fault everyone's always having a go at me.'

She makes an exasperated noise. 'Tell me, is it *extra* making you this whiny? Because if so, the cure can't come fast enough.'

'Oh, bite me.' As a comeback, I admit it's kind of pathetic, as well as giving her an open goal, I belatedly realize. But she doesn't make the obvious reply. Instead, her silence has the smugness of someone making sure we all know who's taking the moral high ground.

I turn to Ben, who's been lying on his side watching us quietly the whole time, but he shuts me down before I've said another word.

'Leave me out of this. I'm getting some sleep.'

Trust Ben to be the grown-up in the room.

I lie back down moodily, turning my back on Elena, and hear the rustle of blankets as she settles herself. Weariness overtakes me, but I can't immediately doze off.

After a few minutes, Elena starts humming quietly to herself, a song that sounds familiar but takes me a few minutes to recognize. It's 'O Kindly Moon', the song we learned as kids, that we sang at school before Confinement Nights. She always told me she hated it. Is she mocking me?

Her voice is silky and sweet. It takes me back to when we were little. When our friendship was simple, easy, fun.

Suddenly I can't bear to be in the same room as her.

I leave my mattress where it is and walk down the landing to the furthest room, a tiny one with a single bed we haven't touched.

I throw myself onto it and fully expect to cry myself to sleep, but it's as though being alone finally allows my mind and body to relax. I feel myself going under, my head sinking deep into the pillow, utterly exhausted.

That's probably why I don't wake up until the man encased in ice is standing right over me.

CHAPTER 22

Monday 11 February –
EARLY MORNING ON HOWL NIGHT

The first thing I'm aware of is a drop in temperature. The top of my head is right next to a warm radiator, but the hairs down my arms have all risen. It's as though a cold draught has blown in, but I certainly didn't open a window last night.

My closed eyelids register it's not totally dark anymore. Dawn has come. But that's not what's woken me.

I open my eyes.

He's leaning over me. Light through the open curtain shows every crag and crevasse of his face, blinding white, glistening, as though on the edge of melting. His eyes are dark sockets with jellied blue irises, pupils like tiny black pebbles peeping out from their depths.

He's wearing the same plaid shirt he had on under his

173

lab coat when I last saw him. The top button is undone, and the material is torn and stretched tight over the thick ice that covers his chest.

It's Owen.

Or rather, it used to be Owen.

Before I can react, his arms reach for me. One frozen hand clamps over my mouth, making me convulse with the shock of the cold. His other hand is round my neck, holding me down.

I can't scream. I can't feel my throat. Numbness crawls up my chin, down to my chest.

He grins with effort, lips apart, his tongue and the inside of his mouth a ghastly, livid crimson, his breath scalding on my cheek.

Then something emerges from under the front of his shirt collar, like a tie that's come to life. Moist, green-grey. It slithers gently up from his clavicle, circles around the back of his neck, then disappears under the collar again, this time at his shoulder.

Barb.

A moving lump in the fabric shows her progress down his upper arm, the tube of her body sliding past his elbow, down the lower arm, towards the cuff of his sleeve, towards that hand that crushes my mouth.

Finally, my brain chemistry fires off a panic mixture and sends it exploding down my veins. I wrench my body sideways and kick up with my legs, jolting him. His grip loosens just enough for me to whip away, throwing myself off the bed, and he topples forward, losing balance.

I lunge for the door but he's quick. A sensation of burning at my wrist as his frozen hand grabs it and yanks back.

Now is the time for a full Rip-out but I'm panicking, my senses misfiring from the sudden awakening, confused by the absence of any scent in the room other than my own. My own adrenaline-fuelled sweat, its minerals and salts, and from him ... nothing. There is no trace of human scent. He is a cold, white wasteland of emptiness.

An itch in my fingertips at last, and I throw everything into it – a single claw razors out from my right middle finger and I twist, swiping at the arm that's holding me. It cuts a line just above his wrist, a slightly crumbling scratch like an ice-skate over a frozen pond, no more – it's enough that he lets go, but he steps forward, his boot crushing my left foot to the floor.

Out of the corner of my eye, a flash of grey-green below me, a sinuous flow as Barb winds swiftly down his leg. I try to yank mine away but his weight has my foot pinned.

Bending instead, I throw myself forward into his torso, a savage cry escaping me, my head bowed and aimed with as much force as I can manage.

I connect, hard, and he's knocked backwards off balance. But his arms whip out and take me down with him. He hits the floor and I fall onto him, wriggling and struggling, twisting to look down at my feet, trying to follow where Barb is. I can't see her.

With a sudden jerk, he pushes me off and then he's sitting on me, his full weight too much for me to do anything other than squirm helplessly. I'm yelling, my voice high and cracked. Elena and Ben must surely come. Unless ... Has he dealt with them already?

Owen has my arms pressed by my sides, his knees pinning mine. He opens his mouth.

'Keep. Still.' It's recognizably Owen's western accent, but groaning, creaking and cracking like the voice of a glacier. 'Don't fight her. Let her taste you.'

A sensation on my chest. A light weight. Something on top of my T-shirt, moving up towards my face, only the thin cotton between it and my skin. Barb's tail is hooked, just at the very tip, around Owen's finger, while she explores.

The front end of her rises into my eyeline, and I get a close-up view of the suckers. Now I see each is surrounded by tiny, razor-sharp hooks that retract and extend as though tasting the air.

I scream, using up all the breath in my lungs until there's nothing left. Belatedly, thick hairs are pushing up along my arms, my face, but it feels like they're in slow motion. It's too late.

She comes closer still, so close that she blurs in my vision, but not yet touching.

Then, without warning, she whips backwards as though shot, landing with a smack against Owen's neck and wrapping herself around and around, vibrating and shivering as though zapped with an electric current.

Owen lifts his weight off me slowly, rises onto one knee, then stands, looking down at me, one hand stroking Barb, whose body is still trembling.

I feel faint with terror and confusion, shifting experimentally, warily, in case Owen goes for me again. He doesn't. He just stands there watching me, nodding. Then, to my astonishment, he holds out a glacial white hand, in a gesture I realize is an offer to help me up. His rasping voice comes again.

'I knew it. *I knew it.*'

The door wrenches open. Over Owen's shoulder I see movement, and a shovel swings into his head, hard, sending him smashing into the wall in a blizzard of ice shards.

CHAPTER 23

Ingrid

This time, the two guys outside Sherman's door don't try to send me away. They eye me suspiciously, but as I approach, one of them opens it, leans inside. He must have called in that I was coming because by the time I get there, Ben's dad is waiting.

I dive right in and tell him I've made some calls and found out a rumour that Ben is in Yojay. I was hoping he'd leap up and head right out there to hunt his son down, but to my surprise he barely acknowledges the information. Just a slight clench of his jaw tells me it means anything to him.

'Are you ready to film some more?' he asks. 'It's all ready for you.'

My heart sinks. 'Shouldn't you go to Yojay? I don't know how long Ben will hang around there.'

'My people will handle it. I've taken the liberty of writing some scripts for you.'

He turns and I have no option but to follow him into the living room. The camera is already set up on a tripod this time, with a proper light.

I have to face the fact: he's not going out. But maybe I can create a few minutes for myself.

'Any chance of a hot drink, first?'

He frowns very slightly, like I'm getting above myself. But then he says, 'Of course.' He heads to the kitchen.

I get busy. It only takes seconds, and when he returns, I'm sitting demurely, adjusting my hair, for all the world like I can't wait to get going.

Ten minutes later, his expression has clouded over with the helpless frustration that can only come from IT problems.

'Something is not working here,' he says, jiggling a USB connector. 'Give me a moment.'

I sigh, patiently. 'Sure. I need the loo, anyway.'

I make sure to close the living room door behind me.

The hallway is empty. The door to the basement steps is right in front. I squeeze the handle down, very gently, and it opens, obligingly silent.

I wait for a second, hardly daring to breathe. How long have I got? Only as long as it might plausibly take me in the loo. I should have claimed stomach problems.

I find the light switch and tiptoe down the concrete

steps, my heart beating so fast and loud I feel sure it must bring him running.

When I reach the bottom of the steps, there are the sacks I glimpsed earlier. They're all labelled *Cobexus*. There's a long list of ingredients in tiny print: nitrogen, potassium, phosphorus … plus a load of things I've never heard of. A large *X* warns the substance is toxic. It seems to be some kind of fertilizer, agricultural maybe.

There's a long table on one side of the room with a pile of papers on it, a chair, and at the other end, a tank. It's about the size of a small microwave, and at first it appears to be empty, other than water and a very white sand. There's a thick lid on top of the tank, with a keyhole set in a plastic knob.

I touch the glass. It's warm. Hot, actually. Inside, nestled on the sand in one corner, is what looks like a small bag of jelly. A translucent greyish blob, no bigger than the palm of my hand. Now that I'm watching closely, I see the sand is shifting slightly, getting pulled into the blob rhythmically, as though being absorbed. It looks as though the bag is … eating it.

What the heck is that?

I raise my phone and take a photo, then record a few seconds of video.

I've never seen anything like it. It's pulsing gently. It's nothing like the creature Sel described from the lab. As I stand there, a feeling of dread slowly comes over me. I get the sense it's watching me back. But it can't be. Whatever it is, it doesn't even have eyes.

My foot kicks something under the table – one of the Cobexus bags, slightly open at the top. Warily, I push it further open with the tip of my finger. As I suspected, it's full of the same white sand-like stuff as in the tank.

Conscious of the time, I turn my attention to the papers on the table. The first page sends a shock all the way up from my feet to the top of my scalp. It tells me what's in the tank.

Sherman's big secret, laid out plainly.

This is the reason he's been bullying people out of Tremorglade, controlling the streets, taking the law into his own hands. It's not just because he's enjoying throwing his weight around. It's because if anyone other than hardcore Alliance loyalists found out about this, it would all be over for him. And he's not even letting *them* down here.

I start taking photos, page after page, not reading, because there's no time. My fingers fumble over the buttons. I'm sweating. There must be a hundred pages of this stuff. I won't be able to get it all.

In the tank are parasite eggs. *Barbaesis veloptera.* Barb's eggs. How on earth has Sherman got hold of them? What does he plan to do with them?

Was that a sound upstairs? Did Sherman just call my name?

I stop taking photos and start sending them, pasting them into the 'family chat' I have with all my friends.

The little wheel symbol goes round and round.

No signal. I need to get back up the stairs.

How long have I been down here?

I take the steps two at a time, blood thumping in my ears.

As I reach the top, the door opens.

Sherman stands there.

'Oops,' I say. 'Thought this was the loo, sorry.' I go to slip past him, heart pounding, but he puts one arm out and bars my way. With the other hand he plucks my phone from my grasp.

His dark eyes check the screen, then flick back to me. His face is inscrutable. Have any of my messages actually sent?

Then he turns it off.

When he speaks, his voice is cold.

'You disappoint me.'

CHAPTER 24

Sel

This is not how I thought today was going to go. The scene is surreal.

We're sitting downstairs in the inn's main room, Ben and I on a cushioned bench by the window, while Owen perches stiffly on a wooden chair the other side of the sticky table, like he's being interviewed for a job. On Owen's insistence, Elena sits further away, at the next table.

I'm struggling to focus on what he's saying, because I'm stunned that he's saying anything at all. When I woke to him attacking me, I thought he was just like those other Frozen Fever victims – incapable of reason, devoid of any remaining humanity. But now, as he sits there, hands clasped in front of him, back straight, dripping occasionally onto the table as the ice re-forms over the huge gash the shovel made in his temple, he's making perfect sense.

'Forgive me for surprising you,' he's saying. 'But I had to know for sure. Sel, you're immune to Frozen Fever. You, too.' He nods towards Ben. 'Barb can't infect you. You would never have let me get close enough to confirm it was true.'

I mean, he's not wrong.

'I suspected it when we fought in the lab, seeing her reaction when she got close to you. But now it's beyond doubt.'

Owen has barely glanced at Elena this whole time, except to tell her to keep her distance and ensure *she* doesn't touch him. Not that she needed persuading.

He leans over the table earnestly. Ben and I instinctively lean away in unison, despite his words. 'Barb has no interest in your blood. Your version of the virus is different – she can't feed on it. Tell me, does anyone else have it?'

I lie smoothly. 'Just us.'

'How are you ... not like *them*? The Frosties?' Elena gestures over her shoulder in the general direction of outside.

Owen turns to her, blinking, as though he'd forgotten she was there. Powdery snow falls from his eyelashes. He brings a hand up to his collarbone, where Barb is nestled under his shirt, just visible in the v of his glacial

184

chest. It's hard to drag my eyes away from her. She's pulsing, rhythmically, as though breathing. But her 'head' end appears to be buried deep in his chest ice, which is churned up in a circle around it, as though she's dug down, then plugged in. I realize, with a jolt, that she is feeding.

He strokes her gently with one white, shimmering finger.

'Because there is only one Barb. As long as she's attached to me, she keeps my brain from deteriorating. I'm still me. Unlike those poor infected people out there.'

'People *you* infected,' Ben says sharply.

Owen closes his eyes briefly, and when they open again a crystal has formed in the corner of one of them. He brushes it from his lashes. Was that … a *tear*?

'Yes. Before I knew what had happened to me. Please believe me. When I left the lab, I could have sworn she was in the box. I could have sworn I closed it with her inside. But when I opened it, it was empty. I panicked, went looking, couldn't understand it. It was only when I started to notice my skin frosting over that I realized, and felt up around my neck, and there she was, hidden under my coat. It's a skill that enables her to survive, I suppose, and I should have known. I never meant to pass on Frozen Fever to anyone. It takes a few seconds of touch – I must have infected those people when I first came here and sat squeezed in round a table to eat. I've been extremely careful ever since.'

'Why did you even steal her in the first place?' Elena says, gesturing impatiently from the next table.

His hand comes up again to touch Barb gently, as though checking she's still there. 'I thought I was doing the right thing. That Gerry was being too cautious. We weren't getting anywhere with finding a cure, or so I thought. I had better ideas. I was an arrogant fool. And now look at me.' He shrugs, and more powdery ice drifts onto his lap. 'I suppose you think I've got what I deserve?'

Elena waves his self-pity away. 'How many people did you infect?' she snaps.

'It can't have been many,' he insists. 'Maybe four? Five? No more than that.'

'Why is there blood at the gate, Owen?'

He shakes his head briefly. 'There was panic once the infections began to show. No one wanted to be near anyone else. They were scrambling to get out. I was hiding by that point, so I didn't see what happened at the gate, but I suppose things got violent.'

'So those Frosties are out there spreading it around right now?'

'No, they can't. Only Barb herself can spread it. And they won't last long. The deterioration in body and brain is fast. The good news is they'll almost certainly die before they can attack and hurt anyone.'

'They looked pretty active when we saw them,' Elena says, shivering.

'Trust me, they don't have long. Hours.'

'Why did you want us to come here?' Ben asks.

'I heard what was happening to you, on the news. First you, Sel, and then Ben. It was obvious that you were being rejected because of your condition. Like me. Once I knew what had happened to me, I realized I would have to hide. You have the same problem. We can help each other. Protect each other.'

Ben frowns sceptically, and catches my eye.

'You want a couple of teenagers to protect you?' scoffs Elena.

'These two are no ordinary teenagers.' He regards her levelly. The rest is unspoken, but his meaning is clear: *unlike you.*

Ben says, 'But I mean, aren't you going to … you know … *die* soon?'

'Eventually. Who knows when? I will last a lot longer than the people I infected. Gerry didn't tell you this, but remember the original Frozen Fever outbreak he mentioned – Annie?'

I nod.

'She was still very much alive when they captured her, and surgically removed Barb. In fact, that's what killed her. No one knows how long she would have lived if they hadn't done that.'

Elena is staring at him through narrowed eyes. 'How did you even know where to find Ben and Sel?'

'I paid one of Sherman's Alliance to send me

information, and to get a message to you, Ben. As for Sel ...
the same person told me they'd followed you going out of
town, until they were stopped by the police. I rang all the
hotels in Hastaville until one confirmed a boy of your age
had checked in there. It *is* just the two of you who have this
mutation, no?' Owen asks again.

I hesitate just a fraction too long this time. 'Yes.'

He notices. Owen smiles, tiny fissures appearing at the
corners of his mouth. 'Okay. If there *is* anyone else, they
should come out here as soon as possible. You of all people
know what happens in these cases. Eventually, those in
power will find a way to confine you, or worse. Just as they
would me. They'd remove Barb and kill me.'

'The thing is ...' Ben says tentatively '... all the same,
you need to hand yourself in.'

Owen stiffens, already shaking his head, icy flakes
showering onto his shoulders like dandruff. But Ben
presses on.

'You can't hide for ever. If you make them go looking,
at some point they'll find you, and then they'll probably
kill you. If you come voluntarily now—'

'You're asking me to sign my own death warrant. I'm
sorry, but the answer is no. Think about what I said. You're
kidding yourselves if you think you'll ever be welcome in
Tremorglade again, or any place around other people.' He
stands up abruptly. 'If you'll excuse me, I need to rest for
a couple of hours.'

We watch him go up the stairs, and an uncomfortable silence descends.

Eventually Elena whispers, 'We tried our best. I say we go before he wakes up, and raise the alarm.'

'We can't give up that easily!' I protest, then lower my voice when she flaps desperately at me. 'We have to convince him. I can't get used to the idea that someone who looks like him still has rational thoughts. Feelings. But he does.'

'I don't buy it,' Elena says. 'Not a bit of it. Come on, guys. You've got used to being able to sniff out people's real emotions, so you're not using your brains. Handy for him.'

Ben makes a face. 'I haven't got used to *anything*, yet. But you're right, he smells of *nothing*. I can't tell if he's lying or not.'

'He could have infected you,' I point out to Elena. 'He didn't.'

She makes a dismissive noise. 'Well, I for one am staying alert. Barb might not have a taste for you, but she's got her eye on me, for sure.' She gives an involuntarily shiver. 'You really think he wants you guys here because he's lonely and outcast and wants bodyguards? I don't buy his story. If everyone left in a hurry, why aren't all the cars gone? They just ran out there into the snow?'

I shift in my seat. 'If they were panicking . . .'

'Seriously? Okay, even if he's genuine, he could have

infected a lot more people than he thinks. If he spent an evening in a full inn, who's to say he didn't pass it to a load of people standing at the bar, or brushing against them in the street, even? We've got to get back and raise the alarm *now*, before this gets out of control.'

'I think I can persuade him to come with us,' I insist. 'This is our best – maybe our only – chance to make sure we get Barb back under lock and key, and get the research going again. If we leave now, we run the risk of never seeing Owen again, and who knows what he might do, desperate and alone? He might start infecting people on purpose. Just give me the rest of the day. It's too late to start for home now, anyway. Tonight's Howl night, and we couldn't be sure of making it home before dusk.'

She hesitates, considering the point, and I press my advantage.

I lower my voice. 'If Owen refuses to come, we'll leave in the morning anyway, spin him some story to get him to stay, and then tell the Probius team exactly where he and Barb are. They'll know what to do, and the authorities will listen to them.'

'I guess.' She stands up. 'In that case, I'm going to see if I can find something to charge my phone. Ben, wanna help?'

Ben looks at me as though for permission. I shrug. 'I'll be fine.'

'Yeah, sure,' he says, and follows her out. 'I hate sitting around.'

When I said it was risky to leave catching Owen to the authorities, that was true. But, if I'm honest, that isn't the main thing on my mind. Owen's right about one thing: people don't want me around. My reputation was already in tatters, but now that Ingrid's video is out there … it's surely burned to the ground.

I need to be the one to bring Barb home. On camera. Preferably gift-wrapped and tied with a bow. Failing that, the next best thing:

Owen has to come with us.

CHAPTER 25

As I reach the top of the stairs in search of Owen, there's an odd sound coming from the bedroom.

Warily, I creep closer, and peek through the slightly open door.

I can just see Owen sitting on the bed, head in his hands. With a shock, I realize he's crying, softly. An icicle detaches from his cheek and breaks on the carpet.

At my gentle knock on the door he suddenly looks up.

'Okay if I come in?'

He nods wordlessly, brushing his arm across his eyes. A habit left over from when his tears didn't just freeze on his cheeks.

I proffer a packet of nuts. 'Hungry?'

'I'm fine.'

I wonder if he eats now. *What* he eats.

Empty fur carcases loom in my mind. Entrails in the snow.

As though at the thought of food, he smacks his lips

together, and a chunk falls from them, revealing scarlet flesh like a wound underneath. Even as I watch, ice crystals begin to re-form over the area, gathering until the surface is smooth.

I settle on the floor cross-legged in front of him, close enough for conversation. Far enough to react if he tries anything.

At the base of his neck, where his collarbone dips, Barb's head end, slightly larger than the rest of her eel-like body, is once again nestled. He runs a finger along the grey-green skin, stroking it, and the body tightens further, squeezing, clinging, as though in defence against any effort to remove it. He scrapes with a gleaming white fingertip at the frosting next to the parasite's head end, and I see the mouth is fastened deep into the flesh there. Barb's jaws are wide open, the muscles around it convulsing. She's clamped onto one of the thick, deep veins inside his neck.

There's that movement of his hand again, a quick touch, a stroke, checking she's still there. Like he's scared she'll slither off and leave him. It makes sense; losing her means death.

Even when she was testing me out, she never completely left him. These two do not want to be parted.

'Owen. Come with us to Probius. They're not like Sequest. And we'll protect you.'

He's already shaking his head. 'Like it or not – and trust me, I don't like it – Barb is the only thing keeping me alive, now, and they would take her. Besides, I don't think you really want a cure.' He smiles with one side of his craggy mouth.

I spread my hands wide. 'I'm not denying that. Being this way has advantages.'

'But it's more than that, isn't it?' He glances to the open door, then back at me, lowering his voice. 'You can be honest with me. Have you had a nibble or two, here and there? Just to feel less alone? You bit someone else, didn't you? Someone you haven't told me about. Who? A friend? The temptation must have been unbearable.'

I shake my head, disgusted. 'No, no, I didn't. I wouldn't.'

He presses on. 'I think Ben could be persuaded he doesn't want a cure, too. If you help him see the potential of what he has.'

I've thought it myself, but hearing it from Owen is jarring. It makes me recoil. In that moment, I realize I don't want to persuade Ben. Or Ingrid. It has to be up to them.

'We're talking about you,' I remind him.

Owen sits back, shrugs. 'To be brutal, there's nothing in it for me, if I come with you. They'll take Barb from me, no matter how much you beg them not to, and I'll die.'

Suddenly, it's as though a lightbulb appears over my head. I can't believe I didn't think of this before.

'Maybe not.' I almost reach out and grab his hands, then can't quite bring myself to. I let them rest on my lap instead. 'Think about it. Ben and I are immune to Frozen

Fever, right? Barb doesn't want to touch us. We're ... incompatible.'

His head shifts slightly, letting me know he's listening.

'So what if *our* blood is a cure for *you*? Or at least the start of one?'

Owen's mouth falls open slightly, revealing the inflamed flesh inside.

'What if we could save you? You'll never know unless you come with us. In fact,' I add, getting into my stride, 'Probius would have every reason to keep you alive. They're going to want a cure for Frozen Fever, aren't they? If this outbreak doesn't fizzle out. They won't remove Barb until they know they can do it safely.'

He says nothing. Impatience fizzes through me.

'Come on. What do you say?'

He's looking away out of the window, into the distance. I bite my lip, holding my breath, resisting the temptation to press him more, in case I ruin it. I really think he's considering it.

Just then, two sets of footsteps clump heavily up the stairs. Elena and Ben returning.

I stand up to head them off at the door before they can break the spell, but I'm not fast enough.

Elena barrels through, already halfway through her news. '... found a repeater and set it up and we *got a signal*!'

She seems excited, but Ben is hot on her heels, and his expression is more ... devastated. He looks sick.

'So I just got a bunch of messages from Ingrid, all at once,' Elena continues, breathlessly, and my mind immediately switches track. In an instant, I forget about Owen. I grab the phone off her and scroll the messages, scanning quickly.

'She's okay!' Elation floods through me.

But Elena holds up a hand. 'Read on.'

The first messages are Ingrid apologizing for the video, explaining. Then she says Sherman's hiding something in his house, and that she's going back the following day to try to take a look. Then, some photos, presumably from today. A tank with something blurry in it. Then snaps of some paperwork. Then nothing. No explanation.

'Those papers are about parasite eggs,' Elena says. 'We zoomed in and read what she sent. It's all information about how to look after them. *Barb's* eggs. Sherman has them.'

My stomach drops.

I glance at Ben. He looks shell-shocked.

'I had no idea,' he says faintly. 'I was so focused on getting away. He never said anything to me. Why would he … I don't understand.'

Elena takes the phone back from me. 'We've tried calling, but she's not answering.'

Dread makes the hairs on my neck stand up.

'Oh no. What if Sherman caught her?'

'Dad won't hurt her,' Ben insists. 'But I do worry about some of those people he's brought in. They're … zealots.

He can't possibly control them all. Let's go back. I'll talk to him.'

'Sherman and the Alliance are the least of your friend's problems.'

We all turn at the sound of Owen's voice. He's standing rigid, hands clutched at the sides of his head, clearly in distress.

'Those eggs. If they are Barb's eggs, they're just as dangerous as Barb is.' He gestures at me and Ben. 'Other than you two, anyone else who touches them will be infected.'

'But Ingrid will be immune,' Ben whips round to me, sounding hopeful. 'Since she's the same as us.'

Owen startles. 'The one in Sherman's house ... she has the mutation?'

Elena brushes past me, angry, as though to get up in Owen's face, then has second thoughts about being too close, and just glares at him. 'Never mind that. How did Sherman get hold of Barb's eggs, *Owen*?'

Owen's jellied eyes are impossible to read, deep in the shadows of their sockets, but he shakes his head vehemently. 'I don't know, I swear! I didn't even know she had laid any! We'd tried in the lab but failed in every attempt. I thought I could do better; that's why I took her. Gerry must have already succeeded alone and kept it a secret. Why would he ... ?' he trails off, and then looks at Ben sharply. 'Gerry must have sold them to your father.'

'Oh, really?' Elena's hands are on her hips, scornful. 'Or did *you*?'

I'm struggling to get my head around this whole egg news. Gerry never mentioned their existence. Did I completely misread him?

I turn to Ben. 'What would your dad want with Barb's eggs? He's the one who needed the research to carry on, more than anyone. He can't possibly think he can do it himself.'

Ben bites his lip. 'Maybe he thinks he's keeping them safe, just for now? He kept on about security after what happened at Probius ...'

'No.' We all turn to Owen, who's straightened up. 'I think I know exactly what he wants with them.' He puts both hands to his neck, gently, and Barb's body tightens round it. 'Sherman wants to cure everyone from Turning, correct? To take the world back to before the Rippocalypse.'

We nod.

'When I was working at the lab, one of my theories was that ingesting Barb's eggs might be a possible cure for *corpus pilori*.'

'Ingesting?' I ask.

'Swallowing them,' Elena explains grimly.

Owen continues, 'The idea being that the parasites would hatch in the patient's digestive system and quickly absorb the virus, *but* that they couldn't survive long in stomach acid, as they do in blood. I felt it was an exciting idea, so I shared it with Gerry. I wrote a report. This may be what Sherman intends to do.'

A nasty, cold sensation is crawling up my spine that has nothing to do with Owen bringing the temperature down. His tongue darts out and sweeps across his upper lip, shockingly vivid against the white.

'No one in their right mind would eat those things,' I say.

'No. You're right. If I were him ... I would put them in Tremorglade's drinking water.'

Ben explodes at this.

'He would *never* – no way. Believe me, he wouldn't!' He stares pleadingly at me and Elena. I catch her eye. It's safe to say neither of us is as confident as he is.

'Just in case ...' I say carefully '... we need to get home ASAP. Hopefully Ingrid isn't in danger of infection from the eggs, but everyone else will be.'

'I will come with you,' Owen says immediately.

My jaw drops open at his sudden change of heart.

'This has gone too far. I need to make it right. I'm your way in – Sherman and his people will scatter when they see me. We'll be able to get to the eggs without resistance.'

As I cast my eye over his frost-ravaged form, I can see he might have a point.

Owen continues, 'The keys to those cars outside are bound to be nearby. The track you came in on is much more direct but impossible to drive. So we'll go the longer way, as Ben did. If you Turn, you can run alongside. If you stay human, you can ride next to me. The girl will be safe here in the meantime.' He gestures to Elena.

Elena's eyebrows shoot up and she exhales a sharp, dismissive laugh. 'Excuse me? We're all going.'

Owen looks surprised. He turns to her. 'But … you can't. It's Howl night. As an ordinary Ripper, you have no control over your actions. You might wander aimlessly for hours into the forests round here.'

'No, no, it's okay,' I tell him. 'She can ride in the car – in the back so she doesn't accidentally touch you. She doesn't Turn yet.'

His eyes widen in astonishment, and he looks first at Elena, then me. 'Oh, but you're wrong. My nostrils are caked with ice and even I can tell. You really have been distracted, haven't you? Give her a sniff.'

All I do is turn my head towards Elena, and the air brings her scent. Instantly, it's obvious. My breath catches.

I can't believe I missed it.

The way she smelled when we were setting out from that shop in Mowbury.

Dammit, she even sang to the moon last night.

Why didn't I put two and two together? I could kick myself.

Dusk is in two hours.

She's going to Turn for the first time.

CHAPTER 26

There's no alternative. And no time to lose.

I gather my stuff from upstairs in the bedroom, as Elena sits quietly on the bed, biting her nails thoughtfully and staring out into the countryside. Ben paces anxiously and keeps telling me his dad would never risk infecting everyone with Frozen Fever just to cure Turning. He's going to stay here with Elena. He at least will be able to use his brain tonight, so he can look after her.

'Maybe so,' she replies. 'But we need to get those eggs. And we need to turn Owen in before he changes his mind.'

I heft my bag and turn to walk out of the room, but she grabs my sleeve. 'Don't go.'

'We've been through this. I have to.'

'I don't trust him. Why does he even want to do this?'

I sigh. 'It was *my* idea to leave.'

'Yeah, but he was suddenly all over it. He's hiding something.'

'I persuaded him, just before you came in and told us

about Ingrid's message and the eggs. I told him mine and Ben's blood might hold a cure for *him*. I think the eggs just clinched it.'

'Oh, great,' Ben puts in, mildly. 'So you put into his head the idea he should try drinking your blood. I'm not sure that was smart.'

'I don't know,' Elena continues. 'I don't like it. Something's going on. Just now, I thought I saw more Frosties out there.'

She nods towards the window and the snow-covered hills dotted with trees beyond.

'Could have been the same ones as before?'

'Maybe. But I thought I saw more. Maybe a dozen. It was hard to tell, they were a long way off, barely dots on the snow.'

I scan the area, but nothing stirs.

'Could it have been animals? A herd of sheep or something?'

'I don't think so. They were running.'

I catch my breath. 'Towards us?' I imagine Owen driving through a crowd of them, like massive hailstones bouncing off the windscreen.

'No, away.'

'Well … that's good, isn't it?' Ben points out.

But she keeps frowning. 'He said he only infected four or five. He said they wouldn't have infected anyone else.'

'I'll be careful, I promise. I won't take my eyes off him.' I take a deep breath, let it out shakily. 'You guys just ... stay inside, right?' I glance at Ben. 'Look, I know this is going to be new to you, too, but you'll have your brain, at least. Elena won't. Make sure she stays in here. Keep the doors and windows shut. Don't go anywhere.'

'I won't.'

'I'm really nervous,' Elena says. She looks pale, fragile. So unlike her usual self.

Ben's hand reaches out for hers. 'Me, too. We'll get through it.'

She laces her fingers through his.

'I'll see if I can stay human too,' Ben says. I smile encouragingly, but I somehow doubt it. It's taken me months to get the control I have, and right now my previous self-confidence that I'll be able to resist Howl night is draining away fast. This is all too much.

A car horn sounds from outside. Owen dropping a hint. I need to get going. There's only an hour or so till dusk.

We all head downstairs and out to the street.

A beat-up old four-wheel-drive is chuntering away right outside, clouds of exhaust billowing. There's a crow standing on the bonnet, cleaning under its wing, but it looks up at my approach, black eyes inscrutable.

Owen sits at the wheel, staring ahead. I can't smell him, but it's obvious he's tense, impatient. He hits the horn again and the crow flies off.

I get in, throw my rucksack onto the back seat, look

back at Elena and Ben's anxious faces. 'See you tomorrow.' Then I shut the door.

» » »

Owen drives fast, unnaturally thick hands squeezed into an old pair of gloves I found, holding the steering wheel tightly. When he put them on, the material ripped on half the fingers, but they're giving him just enough grip to stop us flying out of control. I find myself hanging on to the door handle, occasionally banging my head on the ceiling as the car bounces over potholes hidden under the snow. The track travels miles in the opposite direction from the way we want to go, before slowly looping around and becoming more of a proper road. I glare out of the window at the implacable hills in our way.

I'm worried about the eggs.

But I'm more worried about Ingrid. My phone wouldn't charge – it must have got damaged when I dropped it on the way here – so I've no way of getting hold of her. Maybe I should've asked Elena for hers, since she and Ben won't be able to use it during the night anyway. But I couldn't leave them without one.

I've been watching all around as we drive, but haven't seen any sign of Frosties. They're probably running aimlessly through the countryside. So long as they're doing it in a different direction from us, that's fine. They're a problem for another day.

I check my watch. 'Fifteen minutes to dusk. We should stop just before, so I can get out. Just in case.'

If I do Rip out, the last thing I need is to get stuck between the seat and the dashboard, like a massive furry airbag.

He nods, briefly. 'You think you can do it?'

'No idea,' I admit. 'It's one thing being able to control it the rest of the month, but the pull of the full moon ...' I trail off. I can already feel it close, like there's a strong magnet nearby. Normally, when the moment comes, it just happens, like I'm a liquid being poured into a Ripper-shaped bottle. I've never tried to fight it before. Right now, it seems ridiculous, like trying to stop the tide coming in.

'Now that we're alone, will you be honest?' he says.

'Honest? What do you mean? I've been honest.'

He huffs a small laugh, spinning the wheel around a bend so I thud into the car door.

'About what you really want.'

I glance at him out of the corner of my eye. 'What are you talking about?'

'That's two friends you bit.' He keeps his eyes on the tricky road ahead. We're halfway along the long loop around the hills. 'Ben, and this friend Ingrid.'

'No, I told you, I didn't bite her. We got it at the same time.'

Cracks appear along the cheek that's facing me, as he grins. 'Just like you didn't bite Ben, right?'

'I didn't! Well, technically I did, but not on purpose.' I try to keep the irritation out of my voice.

'You don't need to pretend. I feel the same way.'

'I'm not … Wait, what?'

He shrugs, both hands still on the wheel. 'It took all my willpower not to infect Elena back there, you know. Don't look at me like that. I didn't do it, did I? For your sake. I'm just saying, I understand. You don't need to lie to me.'

Disgust prickles at me. 'Hey, what are you getting at? You think I want everyone to be the same as me?'

'The same, no. But family … everyone wants family. It's only natural.' He chuckles to himself, like he's certain he's got the measure of me. It makes my skin crawl. 'You have a special connection with Ben and Ingrid, don't you?'

'Well, yes, but …'

In front of my eyes, the dashboard clock updates.

'Stop now,' I snap. I almost missed it. There's only one minute till dusk. I need to prepare, if I've got any chance of staying human. Brace myself. If this doesn't work, I'll have to run next to the car. I can do it, but I'll arrive in Tremorglade exhausted. Even Rippers can't run full speed without a break all night.

He pulls the car over, and I get out, the wind biting at my face.

I take a few steps to the side of the road, my gaze drawn to the moon. It's so huge and bright it takes my breath away. Energy and power begin to trickle through my veins. It's as though the light is filling me up.

Thirty seconds.

I glance over at Owen. He leans forward and wipes the fogging windscreen with his glove, then crosses his arms on top of the steering wheel and rests his blockish chin on top, watching me curiously.

His talk has unnerved me. That stuff about being tempted to infect Elena, and insisting that I want to spread *extra*. What's that all about?

Focus.

Here it comes. It feels like I'm watching an enormous wave sweep towards me, blocking out the horizon, feeling the vibrations, the power as it surges. Normally I welcome it. Now, I'm intimidated by it. Its sheer size, its insistence, its strength.

Every hair stands up on my skin.

I brace.

It hits me and I put up a fight, clenching my fists. My claws will slice through my palms if they emerge. The pressure builds quickly, my body filling with extra cells, packed tight, painful, pushing outwards, trying to force my fingers to uncurl, to allow the razor-sharp claws their space. I realize my foolishness, my arrogance. I can't win against this kind of power.

My friends' faces flash in front of me. Elena and Ben, vulnerable, relying on me. Ingrid, in trouble, desperate for a cure. Ingrid has always been so confident physically, a taekwondo champion. If she tried, I bet she could do this. She once told me it didn't matter how powerful your opponent was – you just had to use their strength to your advantage, redirect it.

And just like that, I see the way. I stop trying to push back against the force that wants me to Rip out, and I show it another path instead. Inwards, back to its source.

I'm no longer trying to win against my own body – it feels more like I'm communicating with it. I'm not denying it, I'm negotiating, promising that there will be a time, but it's not now. The pressure instantly eases. My skin stops stretching, hairs retract, the bones in my face stop aching. My body is no longer fighting me.

We're partners. I can trust it, and it trusts me.

CHAPTER 27

Pedro

Dad is downstairs with Jenny, Sel's mum. I can hear their voices rising and falling, making increasingly desperate phone calls and trying to come up with ideas before dusk falls.

After we returned home to Greenvale from yesterday's failed rescue mission, Mika and I finally got a bunch of messages from Ingrid. Then a few more this morning with no explanation – just a photo of something in a tank, and a couple of shots of some paperwork, about caring for parasite eggs. This must be what Sherman's up to, but what he's doing it for, it's impossible to say.

Hearing from Ingrid was a huge relief – I should have had more faith in her. But what she asked of us is proving even more impossible than it first sounded. And what's worrying me now is that she's not answering her phone.

In her first messages, she reckoned she could send Sherman out of Tremorglade on a wild goose chase easily enough by pretending she'd heard a rumour about where Ben was – the problem is all the Alliance people he's got roaming around Tremorglade. Somehow, we're supposed to get rid of *them* so she can get out with the eggs.

I tried ringing Probius, but when I finally got through to someone she denied that any *barbaesis veloptera* eggs exist. Not part of the programme, apparently. The woman on the phone was kind of condescending, like I must have misunderstood. Either she's lying, or the eggs came from somewhere else. I've sent Ingrid's photos to their email address and had an autoreply – I doubt anyone will look at them properly today.

Dad and Jen and I have rung the police in every adjoining area, we've rung government departments, we've even tried to find a phone number for the army. No one seems to grasp that this is urgent. They've never heard anything about missing eggs, only a missing parasite. Maybe I should have lied and told them Barb herself was there. But I doubt even that would have worked – they clearly think we're cranks. And they're reluctant to go up against the Immutable Alliance here, when they know it would aggravate the group's members in their own areas.

At any rate, it seems like they all have their hands full. *Sorry, we are unavailable to assist you at this time. Please leave a message, or submit a request through our website.*

We do, but who knows how long it will take them to pick those up, and identify them as urgent?

The only good news is that the professor from Probius, Gerry, is apparently conscious now, in hospital. Sel reckoned he was a decent guy. So I've rung the hospital and asked them to give him a message that I dictated to them, explaining about the eggs and asking for advice. I can only hope they've actually given it to him, and that he's capable of understanding it and responding.

We're increasingly desperate, running out of time. Dusk is approaching fast – Howl night, when most of us will be as much use as a broken tail.

Mika is prattling away behind me, lying on the floor, propped up on her elbows, her ideas ranging from 'steal a smoke bomb and throw it at them' to 'dress up as one of them and hide me under your coat'. I stopped listening a while ago. I'll send her home to her parents in a minute – only next door.

I'm used to worrying about my sister, and it makes my blood run cold when I picture her out there doing who knows what, putting herself in danger. I might not like it, but it's who she is, and there's nothing I can do for her.

Ingrid, on the other hand, needs my help. Not for the first time, I wonder how Howl nights always manage to land in the middle of crises. I swear, it's like the moon's doing it on purpose.

Mika wants us to go back to Tremorglade first thing

tomorrow and try to get past the goons again. But we're no better off than last time. I point this out to her. We need them to leave.

'But they won't go anywhere without Sherman's say-so,' she sighs.

That's when the answer hits me right between the eyes. I almost fall backwards off my chair.

Quickly, I outline my plan to Mika, and she bounces up and down with delight.

I check the clock. An hour till dusk. An hour before my brain checks out for the night.

'This is going to be tight,' I tell Mika. 'I might need you to press the button to get it online if I'm not fast enough.'

'No probs,' she says, literally vibrating with excitement. 'Hurry up.'

My fingers fly over the keyboard. I try not to look at the clock again, because every time I do, it's moved on too fast.

Sherman's channel finally loads on my screen. The guy's site is so slow.

I crack my knuckles, stretch my fingers. There's nowhere near enough time to do a decent job.

This is not going to be pretty.

It had just better be enough.

CHAPTER 28

Ingrid

I'm sitting in the chair, my wrists and ankles tied to it.

To my left sits the small tank, with its glistening, jelly-like contents nestled at the bottom, submerged in the heated water. I feel the warmth radiating from it on my cheek.

'Beautiful, in their own way, aren't they?' Sherman says. He's just come back down the stairs, having left me here alone for … I don't know how long. I've kind of been zoning out. At least he's put the gun down, now. It's at the far end of the table, well out of my reach.

I don't reply.

'I must say, I'm disappointed in you, Ingrid. I'm going to choose to believe that this was a moment of weakness, rather than that you've been lying to me this whole time. I try to think the best of people. And you've shown flashes of common sense in the past day or so. I don't want to give up on you. I like you. You're not a bad person, unlike Sel and those others.'

I almost laugh at that.

'You're holding me down here at gunpoint. What do you do to people you *don't* like?'

'I'm saving you from yourself.'

I shuffle, moving my arms to the extent the ropes allow, demonstrating the position I'm in. 'Funny way of showing it.'

'You were going to make a mistake, Ingrid. Giving up these eggs to Probius, or to any authorities, at this time would be the worst possible thing you could do. For yourself, and for all of us. They're not ready for them. They don't have the vision to do what needs to be done, to make progress.'

'You're literally stopping progress from happening, Sherman. How do you think they'll be able to do the research that's needed to find a cure without any samples?'

He chuckles. 'That's just it. They've already found the cure, they just won't admit it.' He gestures at the tank. 'These eggs are the answer. The cure for the plague of *corpus pilori*. Once we prove that this works, the government won't be able to deny it. They'll have to roll the cure out across the country. And other countries will follow suit.'

'You can't show they work. Not without proper lab tests – and you've taken them out of the lab.'

214

'They were just *sitting on them*!' he shouts suddenly, making me flinch. 'They would have done nothing! For years! And all that time people would suffer, and lose hope. We won't wait that long.'

'That's just how it is, you can't...' I trail off as he moves to a drawer in the table, slides it open, takes out a pair of surgical gloves, a syringe, a pair of tongs and a tiny paper cup, the type they use to give you pills in in hospital. He lays them out on the table.

A chill creeps up my spine.

My throat closes with dread, because I suddenly have an inkling of what he plans to do. I pull my wrists against the ties, but they're tight. There's a little more give around my ankles. I twist and strain them while he's not looking.

He turns back to me, slipping one hand into a glove, then the other, pulling at the fingertips until they fully fit. He picks up the tongs and the syringe together.

'When I began this, I never dreamed I might have to cure my own son. But then he rejected me.' His face twists in pain, before he composes himself. 'When Ben hears what I've done for you, he will come back.'

Turning to the tank, he takes a key from his pocket and twists something on the lid, then presses down. It opens with a rush of steam.

'I'm going to give you what you really want. You've Turned for the last time.'

Terror and rage fill me. A low buzzing begins in my head. 'Are you kidding? Ben will never speak to you again! He'll see you for what you are! A monster!'

For a moment, I think Sherman's going to lose his temper, but when he speaks, he's so quiet I almost can't hear the words. 'No, I'm one of the few left who isn't a traitor to humanity. Now, shh.'

He lowers the tongs into the water, carefully picks up the sac. Holding it gently under the water, he brings the syringe to it and pushes it in, slowly. He slides the plunger up, barely, perhaps a millimetre, then withdraws it. He lets the sac drop slowly to the bottom of the tank, replaces the lid and turns the key, holding the syringe and the tongs in the other hand.

My heart thuds hard and fast against my ribs. I wriggle my ankles, pulling against the ties. Are they looser? Just a little. I keep working at them, discreetly.

'This is what you want, I know it is. Amidst your lies, that much is true. I can tell.'

My heart is speeding. 'Not like this.'

'You'll thank me, afterwards. I know you don't want to Turn anymore. But you're weak. I'm going to help you.'

He moves to the table, his back almost obscuring my view, but I can just see him pushing the contents of the syringe into the paper cup.

My mind stutters, and I feel I'm dropping down a deep well. I imagine a writhing tangle of parasitic bodies growing more and more numerous inside my digestive system, until they burst out.

'Sherman,' I manage, my voice strangled. 'Don't ... I don't want it. It will kill me. I'll get Frozen Fever. Sel said that's what happens.'

He doesn't reply.

He lays the syringe down. When he turns back to me, he's holding the little cup.

Now I don't bother to hide my struggles against the ties. The chair judders against the floor.

'Don't be afraid – you won't get sick. The man who gave me these is an expert. I had asked him for Barb but he gave me these instead. He told me they can't hatch. The fertilizer I've been feeding them makes them inactive.'

'You can't be sure of that!'

'Enough.'

I struggle away but he's strong. He takes my chin in his other hand, and forces my mouth open, brings the cup to my lips.

'Be brave. You're the first, but you won't be the last. Once we've proved this works, more eggs will go into the water supply. Tremorglade will be the first Ripper-free town. It ends where it started. Appropriate, don't you think?'

I wrench my face aside, but he tightens his grip on my chin, pulling it back towards him until I squeal. There's a sensation of something tiny, cool and jelly-like hitting the inside of my bottom lip. I purse my mouth and try to scoop it out with my tongue, but it's as though it's already alive – it slips behind my teeth, out of reach, and round to my throat. I gag, and with a slick, oozing slither, it's gone. Swallowed.

Finally, Sherman releases my chin, stepping back, watching.

I retch, but nothing comes back up.

I imagine the egg moving down, into my stomach. Is it hatching? Is the creature already sucking at *corpus pilori*, sending messages through my nerves to begin freezing my skin, rotting my organs? My insides seem to itch, but it might be my mind playing tricks.

Slowly, I raise my eyes to meet his, full of loathing.

My hearing pops, my senses hum. For the first time, I'm tempted to let go. The Ripper in me is still alive, for now, snarling and snapping; it wants to tear him apart. *Let me handle this*. Maybe its final act before the egg hatches and kills it. I know it could. Just like it did before to Arty, against my will. The images flash through my brain. The stink of blood, my claws, my teeth tearing and tearing. Except this time it would be my decision to give myself over to it.

Why shouldn't I? I have to stop him. Even if it's too late for me, it isn't too late for everyone else. I have to stop him putting the rest of the eggs in the water supply.

I imagine ice creeping up from my toes to my head, my movements slowing, my mind fracturing.

Then, there it is: I feel the moment of dusk like the toll of a heavy bell in my stomach.

My focus is drawn to Sherman's neck, where his blood rushes through the artery deep within, the sound of its forceful current like white noise. The muscles of my jaw begin to tremble with anticipation.

No.

The beast inside me howls with outrage as I shove it back down. Is it me doing that, or ... is it the parasite egg beginning its work?

I strain against my ties. My wrists are still tightly bound, but I feel a pop against my right ankle. When I glance down, the tie is threadbare. One more yank should break it.

Sherman's staring at his watch, tapping it, then checking his phone. 'It's working!' His expression slowly turns from anxiety to delight. 'Ingrid, you're cured! Dusk has come and gone, and look at you!'

He steps towards me, bends over, tips my chin up, tries to make me look at him, expecting me to be grateful.

'You're fully human. Beautiful. The beast has gone.'

My hands are still bound to the chair; they can do nothing.

But my right leg is free.

That's his mistake.

'I wouldn't be too sure about that,' I tell him.

He only moved to Tremorglade last year. He probably

doesn't know I was youth taekwondo champion three years running. He won't have seen what I can do to a roof tile with my bare foot.

He doesn't see it now, either. But as I put every ounce of my strength into the upward kick, he certainly feels it.

CHAPTER 29

Sel

Owen has been glancing over at me the entire drive since we got going again after dusk. I don't know what he's looking for, but whatever it is, he's not finding it. He's been quiet, since I got back in the car, evidently still human. Subdued, even. There have been no more hints about my trying to spread *extra*. Maybe he's even a little scared of me. He seems lost in thought, anxious.

The scenery is different now, more familiar. I've spotted Hastaville, far down in the valley. We're travelling along the clifftop, following the road towards Tremorglade. It isn't far, now. The forest is up ahead, the dense trees that used to cut us off from the outside world. The deep black of the sky is paling. Dawn must be … maybe an hour away? Less?

'I need to rest.'

He pulls up so suddenly that we both jerk against our seatbelts, and the car's tyres judder and protest against the snow, finally sliding to a halt skewed across the road.

'Are you kidding? We're almost there.'

'Just a few minutes. Please.' To our right, the side of the road leads to a few metres of snow and scrub, then drops away over a cliff. The view is breathtaking. He winds his window open, gazes down towards the dim lights of Hastaville, where the very earliest risers are stirring. 'Beautiful, no?'

A movement high above us through the front windscreen catches my eye. Crows, again – this time a huge flock of them, blackening the sky above as though trying to keep the dawn away.

I try to smother my impatience, and my growing sense of unease. Is he having second thoughts?

He turns to me slowly and says, 'We need to talk.'

My stomach drops. Can I restrain him, if need be? Until the authorities can come and fetch him? I think I could, especially if I Rip out. But I don't want to have to. I say nothing.

Outside, the crows are circling, dropping slowly. They begin to land on the nearby trees. Hundreds of them.

'I have a lot of respect for you, Sel. At first, I wasn't sure what I was dealing with, but I thought I could control you. I see now that I can't.'

My heart beats faster. Elena was right.

The birds have settled now, their plump black bodies covering the branches, but they're eerily silent. Waiting.

'I do understand how you feel, you know. We both need to spread – it's our nature. Without company, we're so lonely. It was a kindness, what you did to your friends. You're the same as us.'

I open my mouth to object but the words die in my throat. Gnawing unease turns to dread.

'What do you mean, *us*?'

It comes out as a whisper.

He doesn't answer, but I see his attention shift away from me.

And then, in my left peripheral vision, I see movement outside the car. Someone's approaching. Several someones. And to the right, on Owen's side. I spin round in my seat – they're behind us, too.

Figures emerge from fog, like ghosts. White faces, arms hanging loosely by their sides. Walking separately but in unison.

The Frosties are arriving.

Owen puts up an icy hand and they halt instantly, swaying slightly.

I have an urge to lock my car door, but don't want to show how afraid I am. Besides, I'm not sure how much good it would do. 'Wow,' I say, far more calmly than I feel. 'You *have* been busy.'

He inclines his head. 'I may have infected a few more than I led you to believe.'

I look around. A few is an understatement. There are hundreds drifting out of the mist, torn clothes hanging off stiff white bodies. Inches from my side of the car, someone who must once have been a youngish man stands, mouth wide open to reveal his swollen red tongue and gums.

'So you're communicating with them,' I say. It's not a question. 'You had them chase us when we arrived at Lenton Barr.'

He dips his head, almost embarrassed. 'Ah, I was just having a little fun. Encouraging you to get a move on. Don't hold it against me.'

'How many are there? Is this all of them?'

Owen laughs. 'Not exactly. I've been picking them up as I go. Mainly just had them keeping an eye on things for me, till now.'

At once, I remember the white figure I saw at the edge of the forest when we were on our way to Hastaville. It must have been one of his victims, set there to watch me. No wonder Owen knew where to send his message. A new fear creeps over me. That was days ago. And so close to Tremorglade. How many are there, how close? Have they gone into the town?

'Most of this group around us are the ex-residents of Lenton Barr,' Owen says conversationally. 'But there are enough left behind to deal with your friends, if necessary. Ben won't be able to protect Elena from all of them.'

'So this is an ambush,' I say, keeping my voice level. I twist to one side then the other, trying to keep my eyes on all the Frosties at once. If I jumped from the car and Turned, I could take some of them. Lots, maybe. But meanwhile, what? Owen sends some kind of telepathic message to attack at Lenton Barr? I play for time, try to come up with a plan. 'You can try to kill me, but I'll take a few of your frosty pals with me.'

He looks deeply offended at that. 'Kill you? I hope there is no need for that. There's no reason to raise the alarm, here. We're just talking. Unfortunately, I did not have all the facts until a few hours ago. Your friend Ingrid having the same mutation as you, for one. If I'd known, I would have kept her well away from Sherman, brought her out as I did with you and Ben. Too late now.'

My gaze snaps back to Owen.

'So you're working for *Sherman*?'

Owen laughs out loud. 'Well, he certainly believes so. He hired me to bring him Barb.'

'But you didn't do that.'

Owen smiles. 'I had a change of heart, after she attached to me in the lab, and then laid her eggs.'

My brain is racing, trying to work out where this is going.

'When I brought him the eggs instead, he was furious

at first, until I explained what they were, and what he could do with them. Then he was very, very keen. And he's looked after them well enough up to now.'

'So what's changed?'

'Your friend Ingrid has got the better of him. She has him tied up. But of course, you knew that. Stop pretending otherwise, Sel. I know you are linked to her. And to Ben. You see exactly what's happening to them. There's no point hiding it anymore.'

For a moment, I'm confused ... and then a spark of hope ignites. He said in the car that I had a special connection to Ingrid and Ben. I thought he was talking about friendship, but he meant it literally. He assumes I can *see* Ingrid and Ben. That I have some kind of telepathic connection to them, just as he's linked to the Frosties.

Maybe I can use that.

Through Owen's open window I can hear a gentle fluttering of wings all around us, a murmur as the crows fidget a little.

'But Ingrid and Sherman are not alone in that room. I have eyes in there, too. Everything they see, I see.'

Is he talking about Sherman's goons? He can't be. They're not Frosties, at least not yet. I search Owen's beady eyes, trying to guess what he means. And then it hits me.

'The eggs?'

Everything they see, I see.

226

'*My* eggs.'

And I know in that moment that Owen is long gone. He's been gone ever since he momentarily lost his grip on that slithering, grey-green creature in the lab.

He smiles, watching me finally understand who I'm talking to.

I swallow down the nausea rising in my throat. 'Barb.'

'As you wish,' Owen's mouth replies. 'We can negotiate directly.'

CHAPTER 30

Ben

Dawn is not too far away now, and we're okay. It's been a tense night, with me terrified that at any moment something bad will happen. But slowly, I've chilled out a little.

Elena is a very funny Ripper, chasing her tail, air-snapping at her reflection in the mirrored wall behind the bar, and worrying at the edge of the swirly carpet with her teeth, pulling the fibres apart. I don't try to stop her. If the worst thing we come out of this with is a bill for the inn carpet, we'll have done all right.

I'm glad of the distraction, keeping an eye on her. I'm trying not to worry about Sel. And Ingrid. And my dad. What has he got himself into now? He always taught me to question everything, and that's stood me in pretty good stead in life. But these days, I feel like he's not so much questioning as grasping at answers, any answers, no matter how lacking the evidence is. It's been awful, watching him keep going down this path. Every time I think he might be starting to come to his senses, he goes back on Facts Unleashed and sees some new thing that makes him angry, and confirms what he already thinks. Everyone on there tells him he's right. What chance do I stand?

And on top of everything, I'm a Ripper. This is pretty weird for me.

I was so scared, earlier. But actually, it's not so bad. I can't do a whole lot of trying stuff out in here – but I do feel surprisingly good. Strong. Positive. I actually love my fur, which is thick and gorgeous. When I put my front paws up on the bar I get a good view of my new face in the reflection. Long nose, golden eyes, zigzag silver stripe down the fur between them. That last is a nice touch and a bit of a mystery, until I remember that's where my scar is, back from when I face-planted off a swing in Year Two. It's so faint now that you can barely see it, but clearly my Ripper body remembers it.

I'm curious to see if I can make any of myself Return, and spend a couple of minutes trying to get my fingers back. There's a kind of blurring at their edges, a blunting of the claws, but it takes a fair bit of effort, and eventually I give up. Like Sel says, I'll probably be able to do it eventually. But right now, I'm kind of enjoying being like this.

My spine tingles as the fur along it rises. My ears flip back. My senses are on alert. Something's wrong.

I look around the room. Elena's fine – wow, that is one *big* hole in the carpet now – and there's nothing else.

I pad over to the other side of the room and bound up onto a banquette by the window.

Nothing. No movement.

I'm about to jump down and write off my feelings as excessive anxiety when I see it.

A gap in the wire fence. A big one. Plenty big enough for someone to come through.

It looks like they've taken bolt cutters to it.

I jump off the banquette and head towards a window at the front, my claws scrabbling. I stand at the glass, my paws on a warm radiator underneath it. There's a good view of the street.

I'm just in time to see about thirty Frosties swarm for the door of the inn.

CHAPTER 31

Sel

Something I once saw in a TV documentary surfaces from the depths of my memory. There are many kinds of parasite, and they can be surprisingly sneaky.

Some can slither into a creature's brain and change its behaviour, to aid their own survival. One tiny shell-like parasite even takes away any sense of fear: the host wanders happily around, unafraid, which of course means it's then eaten by a predator – the parasite's real target.

Others cause the host to eat foods that benefit the parasite. The host slowly wastes away while the parasite grows bigger and stronger, eventually bursting out of its victim to spread further.

Barb, I am now beginning to see, has got all these moves, and more. My every nerve is screaming at me to get out of the car and run.

'In my current circumstances, I am limited.' As Owen's mouth moves, Barb slowly circles his neck. 'These are merely my soldiers. Without more queens like me, we will die out.'

'Your eggs. They're ...'

'Fellow queens – thousands of them – when they hatch. Together, we will build a community again.'

My throat is dry, and my mind fills with horror as the implications of this plan settle on it. Given how many people Owen has already managed to infect, I can only imagine how fast they would spread if thousands of Barbs were let loose.

'So we have a stalemate. You have something of mine, I have something of yours. Either one of us can take away what the other loves, at any moment.'

Finally I understand what she's scared of. This is why she hasn't just killed me, or Ben – she assumes some kind of alarm would go out to Ingrid, who currently has power of life and death over her precious eggs.

If she figures out I'm nothing like her, we're all going to die.

Owen's voice sounds almost fawning. 'I see now that you are a worthy rival. I propose a compromise. Return my eggs to me safely, and we will go far away, to another country, to build our family. You can build yours right here, in Tremorglade. There is room for both of us in the world.'

For a moment, I think I see the world as Barb sees it.

She will do whatever it takes for her kind to survive, to thrive, to spread, piggybacking on thousands, millions of human beings. She thinks that's what I want to do, too: bite my way around Tremorglade and then further afield, spreading *extra pilori* until … well, until what?

A final showdown, probably, between her kind and mine.

'Please. We don't have much time. Hatching will be very soon. Then they must have blood.'

Owen's voice shakes me back to the present. I can't smell any fear on him, but I can hear it in his tone. Which means it's Barb who is afraid. She continues, 'All Ingrid needs to do is stay with the eggs, without touching them, and ensure no one else gets to them. I will send my army into Tremorglade to eliminate Sherman and his Alliance. They only await my command. We may not be able to *infect* Immutables, but my soldiers can certainly kill them.'

'What if I tell Ingrid to destroy the eggs?' I ask, playing for time.

There's a crunching of ice as Owen's jaw tightens, a crumbling of flakes from his chin. 'Then your friends back at Lenton Barr die. And everyone in Tremorglade.'

I consider my options. If I Rip out, I could probably take Owen down, but maybe not before the signal goes out to hurt Elena and Ben. And there's no way I can take down these hundreds of Frosties.

'Okay,' I say. 'It's a deal. She'll stay there.'

He nods. I can still see the place where Ben's shovel gashed his head – the subtle difference in the colour and density of ice there as it has smoothed over.

'But listen. Don't send your soldiers in. You'll get your eggs. There's no need to hurt anyone. Even …' It pains me to say it, but I have to. 'Even Sherman.'

Now that I know Ingrid is unharmed and has Sherman tied up, there's no need to do anything rash down there. No matter what, I don't wish him dead. But I do need to come up with a plan.

Barb doesn't get it. She pulls Owen's frosted brows into a frown. Her body pulses gently, feeding. I picture the *corpus pilori* being sucked up out of him, her poison killing him from the inside, but holding him together so that he can do her will. What a fate.

'Your own people have rejected you. Even those who support you have let you down, tried to stifle your abilities. I know you crave acceptance. Freedom to use your talents without judgement and criticism. So make it happen. Bite them. Infect more of them. Infect Sherman – wouldn't *that* make him change his tune?' She draws Owen's mouth into a smile. 'Embrace it. It's your nature, just as it is mine.'

I make a noncommittal noise, folding my arms. It's cold. Ripping out now would get me warm, at least. The car is chilly, now that the engine's been off for a few minutes and Owen's window is open. I allow an experimental ripple of fur to spring up under my clothes. Not enough to tear them. Just a little extra layer.

These Frozen soldiers are making me nervous. They just stand there, all white and solid, waiting for a command. From behind me, Owen speaks.

'A tiny favour, if you will, before we go on.'

He licks his lips, which drip as the feverish heat of his tongue slides across them, the droplets turning back to icicles before they can fall. He flicks them from his bottom lip with the back of his hand.

'Sure.'

'Tell Ingrid to turn the light off. It's too bright. My eggs don't like it.'

I hesitate. What do I do?

I can't pretend. If Barb can see what's going on there, the light will stay on and she'll know. She'll know I'm not linked to Ingrid or Ben at all. And she'll know she can kill me without putting her eggs in danger.

Then I realize, she's testing me. And I almost fell for it.

It's Howl night. I might be human, but Ingrid won't be.

'Ingrid can't switch the light off with those massive paws.'

Owen turns slowly back to look at me, his expression unreadable.

'Interesting. Look again.'

My breathing is shallow, my heart galloping. Somehow, I've messed up.

'Can't you see, Sel? She's sitting on the floor, cross-legged, reading all the notes about my eggs. As human as human can be.'

The shock must show on my face, because he chuckles. 'It's funny, because *I* can see it.'

'So can I,' I say, though I'm getting a strong sense that the game is up. 'I was just messing with you.'

I should have known. Ingrid didn't want to Turn. She wouldn't practise Ripping out, but of course she'd be practising *not* Ripping out. And *of course* she'd be good at it almost immediately. Of course she would.

'Then you'll know that Sherman has fed her one of my eggs.' Owen's face is unreadable.

Nausea rises in my throat but I keep my voice steady. 'Yep. Stupid of him, but then again he wouldn't understand, would he? That's one lost egg. You don't want any more going missing, do you?'

He shrugs. 'It's not missing. The egg inside her is strong. It will hatch into a queen. It will kill her.'

Barb is lying now. She's wrong. She has to be.

'Shall I tell you what *else* I see?' she continues. 'The view from my soldiers back in Lenton Barr? Bolt cutters, snapping the fence. Through the inn window, your friends. Aw – Elena is chasing her tail. Ben is admiring his reflection behind the bar. Neither of them see us coming.'

A ripple of electricity through my head makes me shudder. Panic. But at the same time, something else. My body offering up its power. The urge to fully Rip out is strong. But I can't do it here. There's no room.

The obvious thing to do would be to get a single set of claws out, and go straight for Barb.

She knows it. 'I wouldn't attack me, if I were you. You've seen how fast I can be.'

I don't have the element of surprise. Something tells me if I don't slice her in half on the first attempt, I won't get another go.

The cold air tingles my skin. 'If anything happens to them,' I tell her, 'I swear I will Rip through you and your army and claw them all to pieces.'

'I can spare a few. Besides, I don't think so.' Barb slithers from his neck, up past his ear, and down the other side before curling back around his throat. 'There is no link between any of you, is there? Because if there were, you'd know you're too late.'

The grin on Owen's face is so wide it cracks his cheeks from ear to ear. Through the window next to him, my view is obscured by Frosties. They're all round the car, several bodies deep.

'Your two friends back in Lenton Barr are dead already, fool. You're alone. But then again, you always have been.'

That does it. Claws spring, fur razors up my arm, and I lunge for Owen's neck. One minute Barb is there, the next she's slithered out of sight under his clothes.

I know she's on him somewhere. She can't leave him.

I slash at him wildly, severing his seatbelt, shredding through his coat, his shirt, his trousers. A noise bubbles up from him, and at first I think he's groaning in pain, but then I realize: he's laughing.

There's a rush of icy air behind me, then several pairs of frozen hands grab my legs, and drag me backwards out of the car in a single, swift movement.

CHAPTER 32

They pile on top of me, pulling at my arms and legs as though trying to separate my limbs from my body. I'm being lifted bodily away from the car.

Now that I'm outside the confined space, I don't need to hold back. I Rip out in an explosion of fur, teeth and claws, with a furious snarl. It's easy, like kicking off slippers.

I lash out at the grasping fingers holding me, at frosted faces, my claws gouging through thick ice. I take a nose clean off one of them, half a chin off another, exposing bone and blackened flesh, but they keep hold of me. I knock one or two aside with a powerful swipe, and they're immediately replaced by more. They drop me to the ground but continue to shove and pull and roll me. I'm slashing and punching at everything in reach with all my strength, a blizzard of ice shards spraying everywhere, but it makes little difference. They don't seem to feel it.

As I kick, flail and try to get up, individually they fall away but by weight of sheer numbers they're stopping me from getting anywhere. Dozens of them leap on top of me, as fast as I can sweep them off. When they fall, they lumber back to their feet and come back for more. They're not actually doing me much damage – they're going to struggle to kill me as a Ripper, even working together. But as more gather on one side of me, shoving and pushing me along the ground, I glimpse through the gaps between legs and realize: they're not trying to.

Slowly but surely, I'm being rolled and shoved closer to the edge, now just a couple of metres away. They're going to tip me over the cliff. Together, they might just manage it.

The sound of a car engine starting up close by brings my thoughts into sharp focus. I can't let Owen get to Tremorglade. There are enough Frosties that no matter how many I put out of action, plenty will follow him there. An army of this size, plus however many are scattered around elsewhere, all obeying Barb's instructions, will be unstoppable.

But no matter how many chunks I rip out of them, I'm not stopping my momentum towards the edge of the cliff.

Something sharp slides into the back of my leg as I roll over it, pressed down hard by Frosty bodies. A piece of broken glass, maybe a bottle tossed from a car, or from a summertime scenic picnic. Drips of red speckle the snow as I bleed. Almost immediately, the Frosties around that leg drop it. They concentrate their efforts on my other leg and arms instead, keeping me moving.

They're avoiding touching my blood.

That's what they're afraid of, not my claws,

I reach out desperately with my left paw, feeling for more glass, and find it. I slam my soft pads onto it, the sharpness prickling against the tough skin, finally piercing it as I push with all my strength.

The nearest Frosty, so iced up that it's impossible to tell what it once was – young, old, male, female – lets go at once as though stung. My paw swipes at its leg, leaving a smear of my blood across the white surface. It cries out with a piercing scream and collapses. Where I touched it, the ice melts with a loud hiss, exposing rotten flesh and crumbling bone, then those dissolve furiously, foaming, as though my blood is a strong acid. Within moments, half the Frosty's leg is gone, disintegrated and trampled underneath the rest of it.

Just then, the ground under my legs disappears as the Frosties holding my ankles give another heave. I've been pushed closer than I thought – I'm right on the edge. I feel my centre of gravity begin to tip down as my body begins to succumb to the inevitable.

Twisting onto my front, I dig both sets of front claws deep into the snow, and feel grass at the tips. I push into the hard ground, barely gaining a hold, trying to pull myself back away from the edge. The Frosties' hands grab at my clothes, my feet, my head, avoiding where the glass has cut me.

There are so many of them at work on me that they're still too strong. I need to use the blood on my paw, but then I'll only be holding on with one. There's no other option

I retract the claws on my bloodied front left paw and release my hold of the ground, half twist round and aim a swipe at the Frosties holding me. They rear back, and for just an instant, there are no hands on me. It's enough. I scramble onto all fours, and slip through the swaying bodies, barging right over those in my path, my explosive momentum carrying me past their grasping fingers.

The red lights of Owen's car are accelerating away from me down the road. I put on all the speed I have, pounding the snow, kicking it up behind me, where the Frosties are already in pursuit. The blood on my paws and leg is already beginning to clot, sealing up. Tiny injuries don't last long on a Ripper. There's no pain, no limp, just strength and power.

I'm gaining, but I need to catch up in the next few seconds, or I'll lose him.

The engine guns. He's seen me in the rear-view mirror.

I give it everything I've got. All my terror, my fear, my rage at the thought of what might have happened to my friends … all of it goes into my muscles.

I'm alongside him. His face turns and our eyes meet.

One leap, and I'm on the car, my claws scratching the

roof, the impact of my body cracking the windscreen, which shatters inwards. The car swerves, skids, and I'm almost thrown off, but I have my claws hooked into the steering wheel.

The car picks up speed – Owen has lost control of it. We hurtle down the bumpy road towards the forest, a scattering of trees becoming more dense on either side. The car just nicks the trunk of a pine and spins away, round and round before hitting another tree on the other side of the road and coming to an immediate halt with a sickening crunch. Owen goes sailing through the windscreen and I'm launched off too, thudding heavily onto the snow next to him.

I leap to my feet and glance back in the direction we came. The horde of Frosties are a couple of hundred metres away, but they're approaching fast.

Owen's legs are bent at an unnatural angle, broken. Anyone else in that state would be going nowhere, but his body has not obeyed normal rules for a while now, and I'm taking no chances.

I'm on him, my back claws cutting gouges all down his chest, my front paws pinning him at the neck. My nose is seeking Barb, my jaws scouring him for her. I don't see her, can't smell her. She's slipped around his back, somewhere. I growl in frustration and pause, become still, hoping to spot movement.

Owen's lying on his back, looking up at me. Half the ice

on his face has fallen away in a chunk, exposing bone with a bare covering of flesh like the last scrap on a chicken drumstick.

Then, there she is. A flash of grey-green parasite slips up out of his shirt, across his cheek and into his ear before I can grab it, as though teasing me.

Barb drags a chuckle from his throat. 'Hide and seek, Sel. Can you find me before they get here?'

I back up the road. The ice soldiers are making fast progress towards us. I don't have long. All my strength, power and speed as a Ripper are not enough. There's only one thing I can do.

Scrambling on all fours, I summon the human in me. My fur blurs, softens, is gone. My milk-white skin. Goosebumps. My clothes are lying somewhere in a torn heap back where I Ripped out.

The car is just behind us, having come to rest at a skewed angle on the road, engine still chugging, steam gently rising from the dented bonnet.

My bare feet are instantly numb as I run up to the car, stumbling and sinking into the snow. Most of the windscreen is nothing more than crumbs of glass, showered all over the bonnet. But there are a couple of larger shards. I grab one, and stagger back to him, drop to my knees, shivering.

'Come out. I'm warning you.'

Owen's throat gurgles with a chuckle. 'Go ahead and

kill him. I'll just transfer to one of them for a while.' His eyes flick briefly to the approaching Frosties. 'Then I'll find a new host. I hear Greenvale is nice this time of year.'

'Last warning,' I say. I hold the glass shard in my fist above him, ready to plunge down.

'You'll have to open up his head to get me,' Owen's mouth says, smiling. 'But you don't have that in you, even now. I thought you were a worthy rival, but you're nothing of the kind. No killer instinct.'

'You're right,' I tell her. 'But you know what I figured out? I don't need one.'

I bring the glass shard down with my right hand, and watch the blood spring up from my own left palm. Then I transfer it and do the same to my right palm. The cuts are deep. My skin is so much thinner as a human. I might have over-done it.

For a moment, I think I see fear deep in those jellied black eyes.

My blood drips onto the ice of Owen's chest and his body jerks in a paroxysm as it drills a deep hole in his chest ice, fizzing and steaming.

A glimpse of olive-green at his ear.

I've got her on the run. Scared.

The Frosties reach the car en masse and divide around it like the sea, headed for me.

I twist Owen's head to the side and clamp my hand over his ear, my blood pouring.

Then there she is, at his nostril. I grab, and this time she's not quick enough.

Her body flails in my hands, but they're slippery with my blood, and she slithers out, jumping high, landing in the snow. She dives under the surface trying to escape, but my Ripper senses weave in amongst my human ones and with pinpoint accuracy I'm on her again, pulling her out of the snow. My hands ache and begin to go numb. I'm losing a lot of blood, but plenty of it is going on her.

The effect is extraordinary. She shivers and vibrates like a pneumatic drill. Droplets of greyish, pus-like liquid well up from her skin and begin to ooze, drizzling between my fingers. I hold her tight, squeezing. The tiny suckers along her body are stretched out straight and trembling, the viscous grey liquid now bubbling up all over her as though she is coming to the boil. It drips over my bleeding hands, pouring onto the snow.

Meanwhile the Frosties stumble, crashing into each other, grunting, hands round each other's necks, teeth in a frenzy tearing chunks of ice off each other. They've entirely forgotten me, no longer under Barb's control, under anyone's control, least of all their own.

I kneel there with Barb clenched in my fist, squeezing, for I don't know how long, till my entire body is blue with the cold, and I can't feel my hands anymore.

Then all at once, the Frosties drop to the ground, unmoving.

I let Barb fall from my grasp, and she lies on the ground limp and still. With an effort, I draw a Ripper claw and slice her into two halves. Grey ooze drizzles from the ends, mixing with the red of my own blood.

I've killed her.

Around me, dead Frosties lie still.

I start to stand, but feel woozy. I'm still bleeding, though it's slowed a lot. My body temperature is dropping dangerously.

The sky has turned from black to grey. Dawn came some time in the last few minutes.

I could Rip out, run, but I don't want to. I'm desperate to get to Ingrid, but now that I know the Frosties are gone, and Sherman is under control, she's not in immediate danger. When I come back into Tremorglade, when I see her, I want to be human.

Besides, I have transport. The car's engine is still rumbling. The bonnet is no longer steaming. The road is straight into Tremorglade from here. I've never driven before, but I reckon I could do it. It's a few miles, down a mostly straight road. I've watched Mum and Pedro, and Owen. How hard can it be?

The car's back doors are frozen shut, and I have to lean over from the front to retrieve my rucksack. I struggle into my spare clothes with clumsy, stiff hands. I'm still bleeding, but I've no more clothes to use as a bandage. I stagger over to where scraps of the Frosties' clothing are lying, torn from their bodies by each other. I find two pieces of cloth and press them to the wounds on my hands, tying them with more strips, trying to avoid looking at the dead Frosties. But there's one that I can't ignore.

Owen is lying in front of the car, right across the road.

Either I risk getting the tyres stuck in the thick snow off road, or I move him.

I choose the latter.

He seems so much smaller, suddenly. The exposed bone on his face has turned yellow, like an ancient skeleton. Much of the ice on him has crumbled away. What flesh is left is blackened, dried up, almost mummified. His chest and legs are sunken, as though his skin is empty. Drawing a deep breath, I take hold of his feet, desperately hoping he won't just fall to pieces.

'She's gone.'

I drop his feet in shock at his voice.

Slowly, I tread round him and kneel next to his face. His arm rises up and his hand grasps my coat feebly. His eyes are pleading.

'I'm sorry. I never meant for …' His voice is barely audible. 'Forgive me …'

As I watch, his nose crumbles into his face.

Without Barb holding him together, his body is collapsing in on itself.

I want to pull away, too grossed out and angry to accept

his apology, but at the same time a flicker of compassion sparks in my chest. He's dying.

He mouths something but no sound comes out. He tries again. 'Your friends ... are alive. Elena. Ben.'

An electric jolt of hope. I stammer, 'And is Ingrid ... ?' I can't bear to say it. Can't bear to think there might be a new Barb inside my friend, about to burst out.

'She won't ... die. Her mutation ... it can't hatch.'

'Are you sure?'

He blinks weakly. 'Barb knew it.'

A huge wave of relief crashes over me. I gently pull back so my coat is released from his hold. His hand falls off at the wrist, and his arm drops to the snow with a wet thud, flattening like the bones have instantly dissolved. A rotten stench rises from him, making me gag.

I look away.

'I have to go.'

'It's ... not over. You know you have to ...'

He's gone before he can finish the sentence.

There's a flutter of wings nearby. A crow lands just a short distance away from me, its glossy feathers stark against the snow, black eyes bold and inquisitive, waiting for me to leave.

It must be hard for them to find food here, in the winter.

More flapping nearby, and a few more crows alight amongst the Frosties, black dots descending onto the white. Hesitant, but braver by the second.

The moment I'm gone, they're going to feast.

I can't stay long, but there's one final thing I can do for Owen.

I remove him from the road, taking several trips. Then I dig a hole in the snow. In the end, I don't know how much of him actually goes in. I don't want to think about it. I never want to do something like that again.

I know what he was trying to say.

There's a tank full of eggs in Tremorglade. Eggs that might be the key to a cure for *corpus pilori*. Eggs that I now know will also turn the world into a living nightmare. Queens, like Barb, ready to hatch.

Barb was wrong: I'm not alone. The link between me and all of my friends is real, regardless of any virus, or mutation, even if it's not telepathic. Our friendship means everything.

Which makes what I have to do next so much worse.

CHAPTER 33

Ingrid

Tuesday 12 February

Dawn comes.

I've spent the entire night as a human. Is that because I was successfully controlling *extra*? Or is it because there's a parasite inside me that stopped me from Turning?

I'm sitting in Sherman's living room, shivering. There's finally no noise from downstairs, where I've tied him up, in the same chair he put me earlier. The door to the basement is locked, for good measure. He's a big guy, but he cried like a baby.

I touch my hand to my face, check my skin temperature. A little chilly. But maybe that's just because the house is cold.

I haven't figured out what to do next. At some point, Sherman's goons will surely knock on the door, expecting to see him. I can't handle them on my own.

After a brief search, I eventually find my phone in the kitchen. I enter my password and am about to go to my messages when I see an icon. A notification from Sherman's channel, Facts Unleashed. A while back, I signed up for updates, just to keep an eye. There's a new video, apparently. I'm about to swipe it away, when I notice when it was posted: last night, three minutes before dusk.

I know for a fact that Sherman was otherwise engaged then, and he's been tied up all night. He doesn't seem the type to hand over control to anyone else. Could it have been scheduled? That doesn't seem his style, either. I click on it. The title of the video is 'HELP ME. UNDER ATTACK'.

My stomach drops. I don't understand. He posted it while I was still tied up in the chair.

Are all his Alliance about to descend on the house? I give myself a second to think. Surely they'd be here by now. They've had all night to come and rescue him.

I press play, and Sherman appears on screen. He's in a completely white room that seems to shimmer around him.

'If you're seeing this video, it means I'm under attack,' he says. 'It's Howl night, and I've been taken from my home. I've escaped and am hiding in an abandoned hut at the edge of the forest outside Tremorglade, on the border of Hastaville. I'm begging you, please come and rescue me. They're going to kill me if they find me.'

That's it. The video's over.

What the...

I leap up, hastily turn the key in the basement door, and start down the stairs. I don't have to go far before I can see Sherman, still restrained where I left him on the chair. He seems to have been asleep, but stirs at the sound of my footsteps. The eggs are still in the tank. Relief rushes through me. I don't wait to hear what he has to say, but retreat straight back up and lock the door again.

It makes no sense.

I replay the video, and then I see it.

The shimmering background. At one point his neck changes shape. His mouth doesn't fit the rhythm of the words he's saying. The whole thing doesn't add up, if you give it a moment's thought.

It's a deepfake, aimed at getting his supporters out of Tremorglade. A fake put together by someone who either wasn't very good at it, or else was in a big hurry.

Pedro.

But surely no one would be fooled for more than a second. You'd have to be really, really dim, or else completely brainwashed to do whatever your leader told you. Or both.

A smile creeps over my face.

I run to the front door, take a deep breath, and open it slowly.

Outside, the street is empty. Even the goons stationed outside seem to have fallen for it.

I step outside, breathing in the fresh air, longing to start walking and not stop until I reach Greenvale. But

I can't leave the eggs. I spent all night poring over the notes about them. There are lots of instructions on how to care for them, the importance of the correct temperature, theories about the circumstances in which they might hatch, what might happen to the eggs under different conditions ... I can't risk moving them.

The notes don't have the answers I need, either. It's all theory. There's nothing that can tell me what will happen to me.

Standing there in the fresh air, weak sun filtering through the clouds, I get back into my phone. I need to make calls. But first, I quickly read through the dozens of messages that have pinged in during the few minutes since dawn.

That's how I get the good news from Elena: it seems there's a good chance I might be immune to Frozen Fever. And Sel is bringing back Owen with Barb attached to him, to hand over to Probius. At least, that's the plan. Elena doesn't trust Owen. Especially since she and Ben were attacked during the night, by people he'd infected. But they're okay.

I'm so proud of them all. And Sel has proved me wrong – putting himself at risk to retrieve Barb. I know he didn't do it for himself.

I think he did it for me.

Now, the calls. I manage to get hold of Sergeant Hale. He sounds bamboozled by most of what I tell him, but says he's coming right over. As the Alliance have suddenly disappeared, it seems he can find some handcuffs for Sherman after all. He reckons he might even be able to borrow a few cops from Hastaville.

Next, I call Pedro and the relief in his voice makes me cry. He can't talk for long – he says the professor from Probius, Gerry, is awake in hospital and he's given instructions on how to get the eggs safely to a new lab. I'm to stay with them until he gets here with the equipment.

I won't be able to relax until Probius have them. If Owen is as flaky as Elena suspects, and runs off again with Barb, these eggs are all we've got.

Just before I go in, something makes me pause. I turn my head, sniffing. A scent, but it's so faint I can't identify it. It comes from the direction of the forest.

It's not a pleasant odour. It smells like something died, and rotted. But I think it's miles away, just carried on the breeze.

I close Sherman's front door and go back to wait in the living room. He's started shouting and cursing at me again from downstairs, but the sound is muffled by the locked door and it's easy to ignore him. He won't have to wait long.

Right now, there's only one thing that matters – giving hope to people, bringing them together. And what's downstairs can do that.

The eggs.

I have to keep them safe.

CHAPTER 34

Sel

I steer carefully into Tremorglade, grateful for the straight road. On my way, I pass more dead Frosties, dozens of them, already melting and falling to pieces. These ones must have been in the forest, awaiting Barb's command.

I'm less than half a mile out of Tremorglade before I stop seeing them. They got close. If I'd taken just a couple more minutes to kill Barb, they'd have reached town.

I stop the car as soon as I reach the first houses, and walk the rest of the way, not confident of my ability to navigate some of the narrow, bendy roads here in what is a pretty big vehicle.

I'm braced for trouble, but there are very few people about, and they walk the streets warily, stopping to whisper in pairs and small groups. Just ordinary people, no one in a balaclava with a gun. They notice me, and watch in silence as I pass. Guess they saw Ingrid's video. We'll have to do some work to get past that.

Maybe it's over? Has Sherman given up and gone away, with his Alliance thugs?

I allow myself the luxury of hoping, just for a moment.

Sherman's front door is unlocked and I walk straight in to the living room. Ingrid's expression on seeing me erases everything that's happened over the past few weeks. I squeeze her in a hug until she gently pulls away. Her eyes take in the rest of me and she takes a step back.

'What on earth happened to you?'

'So much, Ingrid. I got attacked by Frosties this morning – people with Frozen Fever,' I say, in answer to her confused expression. 'You won't believe half of it. But I'm alive.'

'Where's Owen? Elena texted to say you were bringing him in, with Barb.'

I hesitate. 'They're gone. For good.'

'Oh.' Her face falls. 'Just as well I have the eggs safely.'

'I heard. The thing is, Ing—'

'Listen,' she cuts in, 'I'm sorry about the video. It wasn't meant—'

'I know,' I say. 'I get it. My name is going to be mud, though.'

She bites her lip. 'Maybe Jim and Tom can help.'

We both laugh, stupidly, but it feels good.

Over her shoulder, I notice a gun on a low table. She must have taken it from Sherman.

I stroke her hair. 'I need to tell you something, Ing. This is important. Those eggs are dangerous.'

'In the wrong hands, yeah.'

'In any hands. Barb wasn't just any parasite. She took control of Owen, and was linked to all the Frosties. She told me those eggs are special – they're queens, just like her.'

Her brow is creased in confusion. 'The *parasite* told you?'

'Yes. Once they hatch, if they get out they'll spread faster than anyone can stop them. They hijack people's brains, talk to each other. They're clever. Sooner or later they'd find a way to escape.'

Ingrid's shaking her head in frustration. 'Queens? Hijacking brains? You're not making sense.'

'I know it sounds ridiculous. Barb is dead, but it's not over so long as those eggs exist.'

She holds my bandaged hands gently. 'You won't have heard, but that professor, Gerry's awake. He's going to get better. He's already given Pedro instructions on how to get the eggs to Probius safely. He's keen to get to work on them. You said Gerry was a good guy.'

My heart flutters in panic. 'He is a good guy.'

And he'd probably be the first person whose brain they'd take over.

'Well, then,' Ingrid says. 'So it's okay. Hale will be here

in a minute to arrest Sherman. I don't suppose Pedro will be far behind.'

I can't let them take the eggs. Thousands of Barbs waiting to hatch. People don't understand how dangerous they are, how clever. They escaped before, and they'll do it again. They'll wait for their opportunity. Wait for one careless person to make a mistake, and that will be the end of all of us.

Unless I stop it happening.

My eyes flick towards the gun on the table.

She's looking at the bloodstained cloth on my hands again, an odd expression on her face.

'What happened to the people that attacked you?' she asks, quietly.

'Can we talk about this later, Ing? Where are the eggs?'

She hesitates, and for a second I think she won't tell me. Then she says, 'Down in the cellar, in a tank, next to Sherman.'

CHAPTER 35

Ingrid

I'm not fast enough.

Sel has snatched up the gun, and is through the door and down the basement stairs before I can say another word, and all I can do is run after him.

There's a roar from Sherman, still tied to the chair at the far end of the room in front of the tank, thrashing about frantically trying and failing to loosen his bonds, grunting and red-faced with the effort.

Sel ignores him, walks closer to the tank, staring at the eggs inside.

'You filthy animal!' Sherman roars at him. 'Get out of my house! I'll kill you! You'll never be safe again!'

My friend says nothing, but his jaw muscle flexes like he's imagining taking a bite.

'Ignore him,' I beg Sel, scared his anger is going to

make him do something rash, something he can't come back from. 'He'll be in jail soon. Just stay calm.'

Sherman is still struggling, the chair juddering around on the floor with the weight of his body. 'He can't,' he shouts, 'he can't control himself. Look at him! He's a killer! Whose is that blood on your hands, hey? Tell me! Did you kill my son?'

Sel struggles to take the lid off the tank. It doesn't budge.

'What are you doing?' I ask.

He doesn't even look at me, but removes the bandages from his hands one by one, still holding the gun. He throws them to the floor and keeps prising at the lid.

'How do I get this off?' he asks Sherman, who snorts in reply.

Upstairs, the sound of knocking on the front door. Sel whips round, panicked, waving the gun.

'It's okay!' I shout. 'It's Sergeant Hale, remember?'

But Sel points the gun towards the steps. Footsteps are coming down them, a single set. Then Sergeant Hale appears at the bottom. 'Hey! Sel! You're here! Probius are on their way, with an escort from Hastaville police …'

Then he sees what Sel is holding.

'Woah. What are you doing with that, son?'

'He's going to kill me, of course,' Sherman sneers. 'Because I know the truth. He can't have me tell it to the world, can he? After he kills me, you must be my witnesses.'

'He's not going to kill you,' I say, as calmly as I can.

Sherman is still struggling, the chair juddering on the

floor as he throws his weight around. 'Of course he will,' he shouts, 'he can't help himself. Look at him! He's a killer!'

There's a click as Sel readies the gun. I never even thought he knew how, but he's holding it like it comes naturally. There's no sign of the boy who once accidentally tranq'd his teacher.

'Don't, Sel,' I blurt, 'or there's no coming back.'

Sherman talks over me. 'No, do it,' he sneers, slumping back on the chair, panting. He's decided to be a martyr, I realize. He wants to have people talk about him, for ever, as a hero. 'Shoot me. Show everyone who you really are. I'd rather be shot than bitten—'

A gunshot, so loud in the basement that it's like a bomb going off inside my head.

The tank behind Sherman explodes in a shower of tiny glass shards, water gushing over him. He jerks instinctively and the chair tips, crashing him face-first onto the floor. The water pools around him.

I'm screaming, but Sherman is fine, coughing and spluttering and shaking his head free of glass.

When I look round, Sel no longer has the gun. He's picking something up from the floor, gently, in both hands. The egg sac. It's intact. Full of its thousands of eggs. He turns to show them to me.

'These are all that's left of Barb's hive mind. And unless they're destroyed, we'll never be safe.'

He's obviously been through something terrible the

262

past few days, but none of this makes sense. Talking parasites. A hive mind?

Sel's holding the egg sac tightly. It bulges slightly through a gap in his fingers. Upstairs, the sound of more hammering on the front door.

Sherman starts roaring, 'He's making it up!' He appeals to Hale, his face dripping. 'Stop him! The boy has never wanted a cure, everyone knows that. All he's ever wanted is for everyone to be like him.'

Hale blinks, unsure, then spies the gun at his feet. He bends to pick it up, slowly. Sel just watches.

'Kid, put that … stuff down. Others will be down here in a minute. I called for a unit to take Sherman, and sort all this out.' Hale gestures at the tank.

'Exactly,' Sel says, knuckles white around the blob. 'I can't let that happen.'

'Don't do anything stupid,' I beg him. 'Let the experts handle it.'

He shakes his head, face screwed up with tension and frustration. 'I *am* an expert. I've had a *conversation* with this thing. You hear me? I know what it can do. Gerry had no idea what Barb was really capable of.'

'Then explain to him. He doesn't want people hurt any more than you do.'

'You've got to trust me. It's too risky.'

Hale reaches out, his Adam's apple bobbing nervously. 'Why don't you give those to me?'

Sel laughs, a single snort. 'Really? Out of everyone in here, it's you that's most directly at risk. You touch these eggs, and before you know it, they'll turn you into a living ice cube and start telling you what to do.'

Hale glances to me, uncertain.

'Don't touch them,' I agree.

'Well, then,' Hale says carefully, 'maybe just hold on to them, for now. Maybe the warmth of your hands will …'

'They're slippery,' Sel says, murmuring, peering at the tiny spheres, a mixture of fascination and disgust evident in his gaze.

'If you destroy those,' Sherman growls from the floor, 'it won't just be me and the Alliance you have to worry about anymore. The entire world will be after you.'

Hale backs off slightly. 'Everyone just stay calm. I'll go and find something to put them in.'

'Don't worry, I've got something,' Sel says, and lifts his cupped hands as though making an offering to some deity.

Too late, I realize what he's doing. 'No!'

Sel tips the eggs into his mouth.

My heart stops. I watch his throat bob as he swallows, once, twice, grimacing.

I can't believe he actually did it. No discussion, no thought for what anyone else wanted. He's focused on Sherman, his expression defiant, blazing. 'You should be thanking me,' he says, 'but I know you won't.'

Sherman starts roaring, 'Do something!' He appeals

to Hale, to me, his face dripping, trapped under the chair against the floor. 'Make him throw up! Get them out!'

The hammering on the front door becomes more frantic.

I feel winded, as though I've been punched in the chest.

'We need to leave,' Sel says. 'Back door, I think. Come on.' He gestures me to come with him. I step back, shaking my head, and fold my arms, trembling. I can't speak. My eyes sting with tears.

He double takes, and I watch his heart break in front of me. But there's only a second or two's hesitation before he turns towards the basement stairs.

Hale half-steps in front of Sel with the gun, but his hands are trembling so it jumps up and down.

'I'm afraid I can't let you go. Not after what you just did.'

'I know. So I'm really sorry about this—'

His arm is a flash of fur. The gun goes clattering across the room and then Hale is lying on the floor, Sel standing over him, fully human again as though he's never been anything else. Hale is clutching his arm, blood soaking through his shirt, grimacing in pain. Even Sherman shuts up for a moment.

Sel leans over Hale. 'See?' he says, almost tenderly. 'You tried to arrest me, but you couldn't. There are witnesses. So it's not your fault that I got away. Think of it as my thanks for not being a total sell-out after all.'

Hale just lies there clutching his arm, breathing in short bursts.

'What have you done?' I manage. My voice is a whisper. I shove Sel out of the way and examine the injury. 'Give me your T-shirt,' I snap.

He obliges. His chest is filthy and stained with dried blood. Not for the first time, I wonder whose.

I ball the T-shirt up and press it against Hale's wound.

Sel looks down at me. 'He'll be okay. It's shallow, I promise.'

I can't look at him.

Sel's voice is pleading. 'Now no one can accuse him of being on my side. You see? I did it for his sake.'

'So do it to me, then.' I hold out my arm, a challenge. 'Go on.'

He backs away, blinks. 'I . . .' He can't. I knew it. 'There's no need. Your video's enough.'

I hold his gaze for a moment. He's wearing a tortured expression, like he wants to say more. But I've seen, and heard, enough.

Over the sound of battering and shouting upstairs at the front door, I hear myself say, 'You'd better go, before you hurt anyone else.'

And then he's up the stairs and away. I wait a few minutes before I go up, too, and open the front door to the representative from Probius, accompanied by Hastaville police.

CHAPTER 36

Sel

At my house, the key is still under the doormat. Even when it was clear we were targets, neither Mum nor I could ever quite shake the old Tremorglade habits.

As soon as I'm inside the front door, a huge swell of sadness takes my breath away. It's the smell. The laundry powder we use. A little essence of Eddie. The pot-pourri in a bowl by the door. And us. All the molecules we've shed in here over the years, that have defied the vacuuming and wiping. When I leave today, I'll literally be leaving some of myself behind.

My bedroom is in the same mess I left it in; all my stuff will be shipped out to Greenvale soon, I guess. I won't be joining it.

I sit on my rumpled bed one last time. From here, I can see the Torres house opposite. Pedro's bedroom window.

Maybe everyone will come back to Tremorglade, now that Sherman's being arrested. But I don't think so. And even if they do, they won't want me here.

Sherman might have been prevented from causing disaster with those eggs, but the poison he's poured into our community has already changed it beyond his control. I saw it in the way people were looking at me before I left, and even more so now. No matter how many videos Ingrid makes. It will be the same anywhere I go. Me, and anyone tainted by association.

What will people do when they learn I destroyed those eggs? Already, I can see how it's going to play once internet trolls hear about it.

If there's one thing I know, it's that the truth of everything I did won't matter. I've seen how it works; this is not my first rodeo. People will have their opinions, and they'll be passed around, and evolve, and spread, and drown me out. It's not like I look like a trustworthy person anymore, is it? As if I ever have.

It goes round and round in my head, and I still don't know what I could have done differently. My mistakes played a part in what's happened, and I have to take responsibility for that. That doesn't mean I'm going to stick around and take whatever punishment comes from people who don't, or won't listen to my side of the story. I'm already paying for what I've done, and I'll never stop.

Ingrid was right all along. I don't need to – I

can't – persuade people to like me. I just have to behave in a way that I'm proud of.

I'll talk to her, once things have settled. She needs time to understand why I did what I did. Now that she knows she can stop herself Turning, maybe that will be enough. Maybe she won't feel the need to be cured.

Tears well in my eyes.

The sound of a siren somewhere across town rouses me. I can't stay any longer, even if I have nowhere to go.

As I walk towards the front door, I notice a corner of something small and white poking out of the letterbox. I pluck it out, and can't help a wry smile. The SLAY PR logo is on the front. It's yet another postcard from Jim and Tom.

Hi, Sel! At Slay PR we like to do things differently! Last June, we took our company in a new direction and we'd love you to join our team! We think you'd fit in perfectly!

I let out a snort of laughter. First they want to help manage my reputation, now they want to recruit me? These guys just do not give up. I let the postcard drop onto the floor and go to open the door. Then stop, my hand frozen on the handle.

I step back in, pick up the card.

June.

That's when Harold had his bite-fest, and they left town.

A new direction.

You'd fit in perfectly.

Finally, I see what they've been trying to tell me this whole time.

CHAPTER 37

Eddie's asleep next to me, curled into a ball, his little belly rising and falling as he breathes.

I'm lying on my back on my bed, hands clasped on my chest, listening. It's something I practise a lot, these days. I love to tune in to the different sounds around me. My section of the cave is dry, but I can hear water trickling down the walls towards the entrance, where one of the waterfalls is. The scritching of tiny paws, mice busy in the nooks and crannies. A murmured conversation further into the cave. I pass over that – by agreement, we try to give each other privacy – and let it fade. Instead, I focus on a tap-tapping about ten metres above my head. A beak. A crow, I think, trying to break something – a snail shell. There's a mouse here in my room somewhere, too, scratching around. I'm getting better at identifying the other mountain creatures from subtle differences in the sounds they make. It's all about being quiet, not just in your body but in your mind. I could never do that, till I came here. The sounds that used to be overwhelming are now calming. My thoughts have space to sort themselves out.

So I hear Jim coming to my door well before he knocks. Even the sound of his steps is perky, positive. Tom is similar, just a little more organized, less all about the vibes. Tom's the one who sorted our Wi-Fi, fitted the doors and other little luxuries in our mountain hideout. Jim put fairy lights up in the bathrooms.

'Hey.' He grins, holding out a small brown parcel. 'You got mail.' He still has his long blond hair in a ponytail, but he's ditched the fake ears and tail he used to wear. No need for them when you can grow your own whenever you feel like it.

'Thanks, bro.' I take it and chuck it on the bed to open later.

'You want to come help me with the new Canape Carnival campaign? I've already roped Ben in.'

Jim has snagged a big new job for this catering chain that's based way out west where things are more stable, repairing their reputation after a series of unfortunate food-poisoning episodes that they're adamant weren't their fault. He works remotely, of course, and they have no idea he's *extra* or that he's part of an outcast community hidden in the mountains. That's for the best. Jim's really excited about it and I know is hoping I'll get involved and catch the PR bug. His passion is for rehabilitating those who've been unfairly blamed.

I'm one of those rehabilitation projects, and I know he and Tom are trying to counteract some of the online rumours about me. Some of what's being said is technically true – I did destroy Barb's eggs, and I did kill Barb. But some of it definitely isn't.

At the very edge of their jurisdiction, Hastaville police found the remains of hundreds of people suffering from Frozen Fever, scattered there and on towards Tremorglade. It looked like a mass murder. And given that Sherman's Alliance were spotted wandering the forest nearby, claiming that they were looking for their kidnapped leader, they've been charged with those killings. The internet detectives, of course, *know* it must have been me that went on a murderous rampage. The tyre tracks found at the scene match those of the car I drove into Tremorglade, they say. Word is, I set up the Immutable Alliance, to take the heat off me.

To be honest, Slay PR is fighting a losing battle with all that stuff, but I appreciate the effort.

'No, thanks,' I tell Jim. 'I'm just chilling.'

'See you for dinner, then. Later, dude.' He mock-salutes, undaunted, closing the wooden door behind him so it fits snugly back into the rock.

The tapping thrush has gone now but I can hear the

mouse *scritch-scratching* right under my bed, and Eddie hears it too. His little head pops up, ears alert.

'No, you can't have it,' I tell him. He grunts as he lays his head back down on his paws. I pick up the parcel.

The envelope is sticky-taped up to a ridiculous degree and my stubby fingernails are hopeless in the battle to open it. It's not a problem. I draw my finger pad along the edge, watch as a single claw emerges from the delicate skin, razor sharp. It parts the envelope effortlessly. I never tire of testing my control. I'd say I now have pinpoint accuracy. Not that I'm special – most of those here had already figured it out long before I got here. They've been helping each other for months.

When I first met Jim and Tom in Tremorglade, I thought they were a bit of a joke, if I'm honest, but I couldn't have been more wrong. They figured out early on where things were headed with the changes after they were bitten. They knew they wouldn't be welcome once people knew what they were capable of and that being a Ripper once a month along with everyone else was one thing, but being able to control it and use it in normal life – that was scary. So they found this place, adapted it for their needs, and brought everyone who'd been bitten here.

Ben and I have fun hanging out, swimming in the water that pools at the bottom of the waterfalls nearby, shaking the drops off our fur and racing across the crags. I called him as soon as I got here, and he jumped at the chance to join us, make himself a new home and start figuring himself out – who he is, what he wants to be. It's not like there's anything left for him in Tremorglade. Sometimes I catch him in a quiet moment, and I know he's brooding about his dad. No matter how much he likes his new life, there's a part of him that still craves Sherman's approval.

I retract the claw before delving into the envelope. Something soft. As I draw it out, I can't help but smile. Socks, with little cartoon wolves on them.

They're from Mum. I may have left home in a hurry, and definitely hurt her, scared her, drove her to despair. But she's accepted the situation. And apparently her main concern now is that I mustn't have cold feet.

It's too hot to wear socks for a while yet. It's already a warm summer, even up here in the mountains. The snow's gone from our slopes, though there's still some at the peak. We see marmots, foxes, and the occasional mountain goat. From time to time we'll even catch one, but mostly they're quick and smart enough to reach the crags that are inaccessible even to us.

I never imagined I'd be able to say this a few months ago, but life is actually good right now. When I wake up, if I've spent the night outside as I often do, I have an incredible view across the mountains to the west, and down into the tiny hamlet of Applegate where the only residents are Old Pete and his sheep. We have a business arrangement with Pete. He doesn't mind taking in our mail – not that we get much other than parcels from loved ones. He only cares that we leave his sheep alone, which we're happy to do. We grow our own food, mostly, supplemented by a few bits and pieces sent from friends.

We can see Greenvale on clear days, way over in the distance, its bright solar panels glinting in the sunlight. That's where they all are. Mum and Lucas, Elena, Pedro, Mika. Ingrid.

I spend a fair amount of my time as a Ripper – we all do, just because it's easier. Quicker to move around, less stumbling over rocks. In fact the path between us and the valley is extremely difficult to navigate as a human. That's one of the reasons Jim and Tom picked this place. Eddie settled right in when he arrived, via Pete, and he's no longer scared I'll hurt him. He can tell I've learned to control myself, make choices.

If I hurt something, it's because I decide to.

One day, maybe people will decide we're not so bad. Greenvale is coming along nicely as a brand-new town and so far it's peaceful, with Immutables and Turners living alongside each other, but the truth is, if threats come from outside, they'll be vulnerable. They might need help. And we have special skills to offer, after all. Ben's tuned his abilities so finely he seems to have a sixth sense, sometimes, anticipating weather changes, spotting lies, even sniffing out illness. Though he mainly uses it to beat me at cards.

Inevitably, there are rumours about dangerous mutants in the mountains. It doesn't trouble us, though – this area is vast and though there's a new 'sighting' of us every week, it's always many miles away from where we actually are. Sometimes an enthusiastic band of Alliance types get together and go searching for us, but they've never come close, and as the months have gone by, it happens less and less. Sherman's in prison, but he still manages to run his channel from there. It's more popular than ever. One day, not far off, he'll be free. And then we might have a problem.

What would we do if, by some chance, he came up here? Ben says he doesn't want to think about that. I think about it, though. Maybe more than I should. We have unfinished business, as far as I'm concerned.

A tiny part of me would like to see him try.

I do hunt, occasionally. So do the others. My strict rule is that I'll only do it for food, not for thrills.

But I can't deny that it *is* thrilling.

I'm anchored by what Ingrid said about keeping a grip on humanity, and I feel like making rules for yourself is about as human as it gets. Keeping them is how I'll know I'm not losing it. For the first time in my life, I'm trying to be intentional in everything I do. So I've drawn my boundaries and am careful not to step across them. Others have drawn theirs in different places, and that's fine.

The mouse under my bed is chewing my rug. I can hear its teeth chomping, the little scamp.

It took a while for Ingrid to contact me, but I think we're okay, kind of, despite the fact she won't come to live up here. I'm not totally sure she's forgiven me, but I hope she will, eventually. She doesn't think being able to control Turning is the same as being free of it. She's scared that being with us might bring something out of her that she won't be able to put back in.

I don't understand why she prefers to live with a secret like that, down there with people who would fear her if they knew she's the same as us. If they knew she could spread it to them, if she wanted to. They're literally calling it *corpus monstrum* now. So much worse than *extra*. Names matter more than you'd think. They change the way people see you.

Huh, maybe there *is* a point to PR after all, even in this world that's struggling not to fall apart at the seams.

A movement on the floor at the end of the bed catches my eye. The mouse. Eddie's seen it too. He leaps to his feet, glances at me for permission.

'No,' I say.

In the less-than-a-second that it takes me to pounce onto the floor, I'm fully Ripper. My claws make its end quick, painless.

Mine.

Eddie regards me dolefully.

'Just kidding,' I tell him, and lift my paw from the small, still-warm body of the mouse.

Eddie doesn't need to be asked twice. He runs off happily with his prize to his own bed in the corner of the room.

My euphoria, the powerful zing of ecstatic hormones that thrill around my body from the kill, is dampened by a twinge of guilt. Maybe I am stretching my own rules, a little.

But Eddie's eating the mouse, so it *was* technically for food. He thinks I'm okay, and he's a good judge of character. Any time I have doubts, I remember that. And practising my skills keeps me occupied, makes me happy, stops me dwelling on negative things.

Like revenge.

It stops me getting into trouble.

For now, it's enough.

ACKNOWLEDGEMENTS

A million thanks to all the people who have helped create this third instalment of Bite Risk, including:

Kate Shaw, agent extraordinaire; Lucy Pearse and Olive Childs, for editorial genius; the entire team at Simon & Schuster, with a special shout out to Lizzie Irwin for events help.

Jose Real, illustrator, and Sean Williams, designer, for the jaw-droppingly brilliant covers.

My Swag team of fellow authors, for invaluable advice, support, and dodgy GIFs.

The many bloggers, teachers, librarians and booksellers who have championed the series. Special mention for the incredible Tom Griffiths, Jacqui Sydney, Karen Wallee, October Jones, and Rob Crossley – your enthusiasm for children's & YA books, and your commitment to spreading the joys of reading, are so encouraging.

And most of all: Rob, Fraser, and Cameron for unfailing love, multiple draft reading, feedback, and support. I'm so lucky to have you all.

ABOUT THE AUTHOR

S.J. Wills grew up in Chelmsford, Essex, where her parents let her choose any books she wanted from the library. She has worked as a freelance copy-editor since 2003, alongside rediscovering her childhood love: writing her own stories. She lives in Kent with her writer husband, two sons, and a large, bouncing poodle.